Crime of Passion 3

Mimi

Lock Down Publications and Ca$h Presents

Crime of Passion 3

A Novel by *Mimi*

Mimi

Lock Down Publications
P.O. Box 870494
Mesquite, Tx 75187

Visit our website @
www.lockdownpublications.com

Copyright 2019 by Mimi
Crime of Passion 3

Lock Down Publications
Like our page on Facebook: Lock Down Publications @
www.facebook.com/lockdownpublications.ldp
Cover design and layout by: **Dynasty Cover Me**
Book interior design by: **Shawn Walker**
Edited by: **Jill Duska**

Stay Connected with Us!

Text **LOCKDOWN** to 22828 to stay up-to-date with new releases, sneak peaks, contests and more…

Thank you.

Acknowledgements

To the many women and men who have passed from domestic violence. I stand with you and your families. To the survivors, keep surviving, every day gets better. To the ones who are still fighting to get out, you will, and keep fighting.

Thank you to all individuals who took the time out to read this book. I put my blood, sweat, and tears into this one. It was a rough story to write because this was my story. Thank you to you.

Thank you to everyone who is supporting me on my journey.
Be blessed!
~Mimi

Part One:

The Calm before the Storm

Mimi

Chapter One
2003

Last night I prayed on a fallen star
That you never have a broken heart
Though the world is cold, just remember
Who you are

"It's a girl!" Dr. Jeena exclaimed as she placed my baby girl onto my chest. The tears cascaded down my face as I listened to her wails and watched the nurses clean her off. Briefly, I took my eyes from my daughter to look for my mom, the only family that I had in the delivery room with me. In a blur, she zoomed past the bed, behind the nurses, and exited the room with tears in her eyes, heartbroken. The nurses whisked my baby away and I couldn't help but feel the emptiness in my chest as I watched my mother exit the room. With the oxygen mask still on my face, the doctor instructed me to push again. My eyes grew wide and I looked at her, still between my legs.

"Why? Is there another one?" I asked.

Dr. Jeena giggled behind her face mask and looked at me. She said, "No, Ms. Richards. We have to get the placenta sack out. You will feel a little pressure. Nothing to worry about."

Nothing to worry about, huh? At sixteen, I had just become a mother and I possibly could have just ruined what little bit of a good relationship I had with my mother. Dr. Jeena went on to explain that I had a small tear while I was delivering my daughter that would need a few stiches. Too much was going on around me. I just wanted to eat and sleep. Nurses were explaining that they were taking my baby to the nursery, the doctor was asking me if I wanted to contact the father, and my mind was still wondering where my mother went. When

Dr. Jeena was done, the nurses cleaned me up down there, placed these bigass pads and mesh panties on me, and told me that I was going to be getting moved to another room soon.

"Where's my mom?" I asked the only available nurse that was still in the room.

"She didn't come tell you?" she asked.

"No. Tell me what?"

"She said that she had to be back to work. She said that she'll be back up when her second shift ended."

Nodding my head, I turned over to my side and let my mind wander. Just a week ago, my mother found out that I was pregnant. Yes, my mother. I knew for the longest that I was pregnant, but I was in denial and walked around saying that I had a tumor.

At fifteen, I was pregnant, and I thought that I was doing a good job at hiding it. My older sister, Thomasina, knew. I don't know how, but she did. She kept telling my mom that I was pregnant even before I knew for sure. My mother denied it, but she listened to my sister and took me to the doctor. They did a pregnancy test through bloodwork and told us to call back in a few days for the results.

My sister wasn't my only sibling. Altogether, I had six siblings. Thomasina got pregnant and no one blinked an eye. She had a baby shower and all. Just two years ago, she had given birth to her second child, which by the way she hid most of the pregnancy. And I knew, but I didn't say anything. I guess karma came back and bit me on the ass when my sister knew that I was.

Days passed, and my mom called the doctor back. They told her that they couldn't tell her anything and that I had to give them a call to get my results. To say my mother was heated was an understatement. She flipped her shit and made me call them. Needless to say, the test results came back negative. Relaying that message to my mom was both a relief and heartbreaking. She didn't believe me when I told her that they were negative. At that time, I didn't know that I was pregnant, but if they said that they were negative, then who the hell was I to argue with that? I was thinking to myself that I had dodged a bullet. As time went on, I got bigger and I did everything to hide it. My mom had even gotten over the test result fiasco.

When I began to feel my baby moving in my stomach, I never thought it was my baby. I was fifteen. In my mind, I was old enough to be having sex, but no way was there a baby growing inside of me. My first thought was that it was a tumor. No one listened to me. No one took me to the doctor to make sure that I was good. So, I left it alone.

Halloween, 2003, I was supposed to take my little brother to go trick or treating when he got out of school. That day, I also had a doctor's appointment. My mom was finally listening to me. Thomasina had to take me just to get checked in and my mother was coming after she finished the first half of her shift. She was a school crossing guard and she had two shifts, one in the morning and the other in the afternoon.

When my mother arrived, we were still waiting to get called. Thomasina left and went home and soon after, they called me to one of the back rooms. Nervousness kicked in because I didn't know what to expect.

"What brings you in today?" the nurse asked, resting her hip against the sink. My mom sat on the only chair available and I sat on the exam table.

"She needs a physical," my mother answered.

The nurse nodded her head and began to ask my mother the usual questions that they needed to ask. They checked my weight and blood pressure.

"Lie down on your back," the nurse said gently. I did as I was instructed and my shirt was lifted up. I looked towards my mother and her face was frozen in shock.

"It's a tumor, isn't it?" I asked. I continued, "Do I need to get surgery?"

I was in panic mode. The doctor had come inside and was just as stunned as everybody in the room. My mother's face soon became a mask of anger.

"Ms. Richards, did you know that your daughter was pregnant?" the doctor asked.

"Pregnant?" I asked in shock as I tried to sit up. My mother forced me to stay down by pressing me down by my shoulder.

"I didn't know that Korrin was pregnant. Months ago, I took her to get blood work done and they wouldn't give me any information. They told me that she would have to call to get the results. She told me that the results were negative. I guess somebody lied."

"But Mama, I didn't. I told you what they told me."

The doctor noticed how thick the tension had gotten inside of the room and decided to speak up. He said, "That's neither here nor there. The fact of the matter is that there is a baby on the way. According to when Korrin had her last period, she should be due in another two weeks. I will get an ultrasound done, just to check the baby to make sure that everything is okay."

I nodded my head and looked at the wall. The nurse and doctor left the room, leaving me with my mother. The room was eerily quiet and I dared not look at my mother. I knew she was fuming and I knew she was trying to keep her composure because we were in the doctor's office. But once we got home, World War III would commence.

"You know you not keeping that damn baby, right?" my mother asked me with attitude stuck in the pit of her throat.

"What? What do you mean by I can't keep my baby?" I asked, now copping my own attitude. She was getting ready to respond when the nurse came in the room with the ultrasound machine. My mom couldn't even look my way. If she thought this was frustrating for her, how did she think I was feeling? She just told me that I couldn't keep my baby and failed to give me a reason as to why. The nurse completed our appointment, so I got dressed and followed my mom out of the room. She made me another appointment and flew out of the clinic.

My heart broke. I never wanted to hurt my mother. I never wanted to get pregnant, and I definitely didn't want to get rid of my child. The walk home was a quick one, but my mind was circling all over the place. I had no business getting pregnant at fifteen. Shit, I had no right having sex, but what could I do about it? It's not like I was going to be able to go back into the past and change anything. Whatever was done, was done. In a few days I was turning sixteen not an adult, but fully capable of making my own decisions, and it was final. I was keeping my child, and that was it.

When I got home, my mother and sister were sitting in the kitchen chit chatting, but got quiet when they noticed I had entered the house. My sister looked my way and shook her head. I know this bitch ain't judging me, I thought to myself.

"Korrin, get over here," my mother called from the kitchen.

Rolling my eyes, I made my way into the kitchen. "Yes?" I asked.

"I called my sister down in Louisiana. She's going to adopt your baby until you could take care of it yourself."

"Wait. What? I'm not sending my baby to Louisiana. I won't ever get it back."

"It's not up for debate."

"Why I got to send my baby off when you didn't send Thomasina's child off when she got pregnant? That ain't fair!"

Thomasina jumped in and said, "This ain't about me, so don't make it."

"Do you even know who the father is?" my mother asked.

"Wow. Yes, I do."

"Is he planning on being there for you or his child?"

"He doesn't know. I stopped talking to him a few months ago."

"Korrin, just get out of my face."

Angry, I walked away and went into my room. I shed my clothes, climbed into my bed, and got under the covers. My eyes burned with tears that rimmed my eyes. For sure, she wasn't making me get rid of my baby. I'd become homeless and struggle to take care of myself and my child before I allowed her to make such a drastic decision for me.

A week later...

Pain in my lower back and stomach woke me from my sleep. The sun was just starting to peek out. My body rocked with pain and I yelled, sliding out of my bed and onto the floor. My little sister, Tahjae, popped up from her sleep and turned the light on.

"Korrin, are you okay?" she asked, rushing to my side.

"Go get Mommy," I said as the pain began to let up.

Tahjae ran out of the room and came back with my mother. A scowl rested on her face as she looked at me lying on the floor. She shook her head and turned to walk away.

"Ma!" Tahjae called after her.

"Thomasina, I'll be back! This bitch is going into labor!" I heard my mother yell.

At the hospital, they had me hooked up to all types of machines. I wasn't fully dilated and I was ready for them to send my ass home. Instead, they gave me an I.V. filled with Pitocin to strengthen my contractions. From that moment, that's when everything with my mother went downhill.

Mimi

Chapter Two

That feeling when you're not necessarily sad,
But you just feel really empty
~Anonymous

Once I was in the recovery room, I had taken a nap until they brought me my daughter. She was all cleaned up and it was time for her to eat. I wasn't an expert at being a mother, but due to all of the times Thomasina wanted me to babysit my nephews, I knew how to care for a baby. Even though I was exhausted, I managed to feed her, change her, and put her back to sleep. The nurse had come back to take her away for testing and informed me that she would bring her back when it was time for her to eat again. It gave me time to call her father.

"Hello?" he answered.

"Hey, it's Korrin."

There was a pause and then he said, "Oh. What's up? I haven't heard from you in a while."

"Yeah, I know. Listen, I only called to tell you that I had your daughter. I'm in Methodist Hospital and she was born a few hours ago."

"My daughter? How are you so sure that she's mine?"

"What do you mean, Raheem? You were the only one that I was with for the past year and a half."

"Yeah. But how that look that I haven't spoken to you in the last four months, and you just mysteriously call me talking about a baby?"

I sighed and rubbed my right temple. I said, "I get where you're coming from. I'm absolutely sure that she is your child. I only called because I need something for her in order to leave the hospital. You can also come up to see her."

There was another pause before he responded, "Give me the phone number that you are calling from and I'll call you back in a few and I'll let you know what I could do."

"7185552901. Thank you, Raheem. I really appreciate it." With that I hung up, and my mother walked inside of the room. In followed her best friend Vera. I greeted them both, but my mom's face looked like she didn't want to be there at all.

"Did you see or hold the baby yet?" my mother asked snidely. I knew why she was asking. While we were on our way to the hospital, she told me not to do either. She said that it would only make me want to keep her more. She's been pregnant seven times. How does she not know that feeling comes before you give birth?

"Yes."

"Why would you do that? I specifically told you not to," my mother nagged.

"Oh, Samantha, hush. Leave the girl alone. Korrin, did you name her yet?" Ms. Vera stated. When she took up for me, I wanted to stick my tongue out at my mom. She sat off in the corner meanmugging me.

"Her name is Iyana. Oh, and look, here she comes," I respond loud and proud just to get on my mom's nerves.

The nurse pushed Iyana inside of my room in the bassinet with a smile. She told me that under the bassinet was bottles, diapers, and blankets for the baby. She left the room as fast as she came in. Ms. Vera and my mom peered inside of the bassinet. Slowly, I noticed my mom's face soften.

"Can I hold her?" Ms. Vera asked.

"Yes. Of course you can."

Without hesitation, Ms. Vera grabbed Iyana up in her arms and instantly fell in love with her. My mother and Ms. Vera didn't stay too long, but it was long enough to hold my daughter and smile. Maybe after all she could warm up to me having a child. With promises of coming the next day, my mom and Ms. Vera left.

The next day, I woke up bright and early. This was my last day in the hospital and I couldn't have been happier. The following day I was leaving to go home and finally get some real food. After breakfast, I decided to call Raheem due to him not calling me back the previous day.

"Hello," he responded. Raheem was always an early bird, so I knew that he would be up.

"Hey. It's Korrin. Um, I was calling because you didn't call me back yesterday and today is my last day in the hospital," I expressed.

What he said next, I was not prepared for, "Look, Korrin, there is nothing that I can do to help you. At least not until I get a DNA test. I'm sorry, Korrin."

My heart shattered. The only person that I thought I could rely on was being a dick. He knew that he was the only one I had been with. Trying to keep my cool, I still managed to yell, "What the fuck do you mean? She's your baby and you just gonna leave me out to dry! I came to you, her father, because she needed a couple of things for her to leave the hospital and you can't even help with a onesie, at least! I fucking hate you!"

"Korrin, you can say that you had only been with me all you want to, but I need a DNA test just so that I can make sure."

"Fuck you!" I yelled. I hung the phone up. I couldn't do anything except break down. I had no money, the father of my child didn't and wasn't going to help me. My mother hated my guts at this point. My body shook as I cried hard. I cried like a baby because who was actually going to be in my corner? Yes, I could have taken my mother up with sending my child to my aunt, but I also knew that I would never see her again. Iyana was sleeping but with my crying, I knew she was bound to wake up. Lying on my side, I slowly drifted into a slumber. This surely wasn't what my life was going to become.

An hour later, I woke up to Iyana crying. I rolled over and grabbed her from her bassinet and unwrapped her from her blanket. As I changed her diaper, I couldn't help but think that she was the most perfect thing in this world and the only thing that made sense in my life. Making sure that she was nice and dry, I grabbed a bottle from under the bassinet and began to feed her. The conversation between myself and Raheem played in my mind and the tears started again. The only person that I could call for help would be my mother, but that would be like pulling teeth. She would only give me a hard time.

"Knock! Knock!" a woman's voice said, coming from the other side of my curtain. When she appeared, I wondered what she could possibly want with me. She was an older white woman in dark brown pants, a white shirt, and a light brown blazer.

"Yes?" I questioned.

"Hi, Korrin. My name is Amanda and I am a social worker here at the hospital," she stated. I noticed the folder in her hands and looked at her face. I didn't know much, but hearing the words social worker wasn't a good thing.

"Okay," I answered with skepticism.

"I am here because tomorrow is supposed to be your last day, but you might have to be here a little while longer. Just another day or two."

"Why?" I was completely confused. I knew from my sister that when having kids, they kept you for three days, tops. The only way you were staying longer could be because there is something wrong with the baby or if you hadn't pooped yet.

20

"When was the last time you spoke to your mom, sweetie?"

"Yesterday when she was here. Wwhy? What's going on?"

The look on her face went from smirking to sad quickly as she made her way to the end of the hospital bed and sat on it. She said, "Your mother came up here this morning and left a letter. It explains that, in short, you aren't allowed to go back home and that we are allowed to find you a home for you and Iyana to go to. I'm sorry that you had to find out this way. She said that the only way you would be able to come home would be if you left Iyana here to be put up for adoption. I know that in your heart, you don't want to do that, so we are going to do everything in our power to find a place for you and your daughter. I'll be in touch."

Amanda gave me a sympathy smirk as she left the room. My stomach twisted in knots as I pondered what the fuck this woman just told me. Is my mother that mad at me that she really went that low to say I couldn't come back home? The realization of not having anyone hit me like a ton of bricks. While my sister was there with not one, but two kids, I was the one who couldn't come home. Iyana was sleeping in my arms. My tears, which seemed like they were never ending, fell softly onto her face. There was a growing feeling in my gut that my sister was behind this.

***

Around eight o' clock that night, I could hear my "roommate" packing her stuff up to get ready to leave. She had her curtain pulled back and her baby was all snuggled in his car seat. My curtain wasn't fully open, but I closed it all the way to give them some privacy.

"Excuse me," I heard. It was from the woman. I'd never spoken to her the whole time we were sharing a room.

"Yes?" I asked, pulling my curtain back.

"I don't want to seem like me and my husband were being nosy. But we overheard everything that has been going on and we figured that we could do something to help you out. I am sorry that you are going through all that you are going through, and we hope that everything works out for you," she said. She handed me a few shopping bags from the children's store Cookies.

I thanked her with tears in my eyes and gave her and her husband a hug. They grabbed up their things and left. I sat back on the bed and looked through the bags. There were bottles, bibs, onesies, outfits, pacifiers, and socks. In an envelope was a card congratulating me on my new bundle of joy. Sixty dollars was stuffed inside of the card and I wished they were there so that I could hug them and thank them again.

In a world full of hope and good people, I still felt empty. All I wanted was to have my family behind me. This was a feeling that I never wanted to feel ever again.

Chapter Three

Four months later

I thought I had it all figured out
I needed time away to work it out
And now that I've learned what it's all about
And all I need is you in my life

Four months had passed since my mother up and left me for dead inside of that hospital. Amanda had come back the next day to let me know that there was a maternity home that helped unwed mothers, which was willing to accept me and Iyana. Wanting to get out of the hospital and not being able to go home, I had no choice but to go.

Everything was all good when I first got there. I had six weeks probation. Good; I was in no rush to leave and go visit anyone at home. It was made loud and clear that I wasn't welcome there. I had to get tutoring for my GED because I had stopped going to school way before I got pregnant. Other rules that I had to abide by were attending bible study, church, chores, and making dinner for everyone, which was all fine and dandy.

Being there wasn't all that bad until my six weeks probation was up, and if I wasn't making a trip to the doctor's office or to the corner store, I still needed an escort with me. Granted, I wasn't making trips home, but the weather was getting nice and the other mothers and I wanted to take trips to the park. Mothers started to leave because they couldn't deal with it. It was so bad that I was left in the house by myself.

There was a livein person who we called Ms. Diane. It was just us and it was cool for a while, until she started to refer to herself as Iyana's grandmother. I let it slide the first time but

23

the second time, I wasn't going to let it slide. A huge argument began, and I was ready to beat this lady's ass. Ms. Diane ended up calling the director and my "eviction" was pretty evident. My bags were packed by the time she had gotten there. My mind was made up, even though Ms. Susan tried to get me to stay. After she realized that her pleas were falling on deaf ears, she began to help me bring my things to the van. Without warning, I was back at my mother's in Red Hook. I left Ms. Susan downstairs while I brought Iyana upstairs. Thomasina answered the door in shock.

"Here, watch her right quick. I gotta grab my stuff from downstairs," I said angrily. I brushed passed Thomasina to grab the shopping cart. Thomasina looked on while holding Iyana in her car seat. By the time I made it back downstairs, Ms. Susan was gone, and my shit was sitting on the sidewalk. I packed the shopping cart with all of my belongings and began to lug it up three flights of stairs.

"What are you doing here?" my sister asked. She had placed Iyana in the living room where my younger siblings Tahjae, Steven, and Elijah were looking at her, playing with her.

"Where is Mommy?" I asked instead.

"She's in Louisiana. Grandma passed away," she responded.

"What? And nobody told me? I call here every other day. Who did she go with?"

"Charles and her boyfriend Paul are with her. You know that she is not going to like that you came back."

I eyed Thomasina because I knew that it was her that was going to have an issue with me being there. I had already gotten the scoop from Tahjae that Thomasina was behind my mother getting rid of me. I simply answered, "I'll talk to her when she gets back."

My mother wasn't due back until the end of the week. I just had to keep it together until then. I was basically forcing my way back in. She would have no choice but to allow me to stay. I needed to speak with her without Thomasina around. That was the plan for when my mom came back.

***

The day my mother came back, my nerves were a wreck. Both Thomasina and I stayed out of each other's way for the most part, but she was warming up to Iyana. If I was in the kitchen warming Iyana a bottle for dinner, she would come in and pick her up to play with her until her bottle was done.

When my mom came inside of the house, I was in my old bedroom, reading a book while Iyana napped. My bedroom door swung open and she stood there with her hands on her hips. I'm pretty sure that Thomasina done already got in her two cents before I got a chance to defend myself.

"You're going to get a job and you are going to put that boy on child support. Until you are able to get a job and take care of Iyana the way she is supposed to get taken care of, I will take temporary custody of her. Do you understand?" she stated.

"Yes," I responded, confused. I was prepared to get cursed out. She said what she said and left my room. The next day, the process for my mother to get temporary custody of Iyana started. For months, until Iyana was one, we went back and forth to court for my mom to get awarded custody. Once that was done, she began to file papers for Raheem to pay child support. The judge granted him a paternity test and upon the DNA test results proving that he was Iyana's father, he would have to pay child support.

By the time everything was settled, Iyana was almost two. My world turned upside down, just as I thought everything was going in my favor.

"Korrin!" my mother called me from her room. I was about to be on my way out the door to go meet my friend Rocky and I was just about done getting dressed.

"Yes?"

"What the fuck is this?" she asked, handing me a piece of paper. I grabbed the paper from her hand and my heart slammed in my chest.

"But…I thought "

"You thought what? You were so sure that boy was Iyana's father, but that paper says otherwise. Who the fuck is her father, Korrin?"

My mind raced as I tried to piece together this mess. Then it hit me. One day I was walking home through the projects and he had approached me. I knew who he was. Every female in the hood wanted him because he was "the finest young nigga" walking in the hood. Even the grown bitches wanted him. Me, it wasn't the same. I wasn't throwing myself at him or any other dude in Red Hook. And I think that's why he pursued me. One thing led to another, and I guess Iyana happened.

"Jaquan is her father."

"Jaquan? You talking about Charity's brother?"

I nodded my head. This couldn't have come at a worse time. This dude just married and the girl he got married to, I went to junior high school with and I just recently found out that at the time I had a onenight stand, he was with her then. My mother wasn't too pleased, but shit, neither was I. Besides being with Raheem, Jaquan was for sure the only other dude I'd been with. And it wasn't too memorable if I forgot it.

"I'm gonna tell him!" I managed to say.

"When?" my mother asked. She was sipping on a Budweiser, ogling me like she didn't trust me to do it.

"In the morning. Right now, I'm going to meet Rocky."

"What about Iyana?"

"Mama, she's asleep and Tahjae knows to call me if she wakes up. I'm only going to be in front of Charity's building anyhow."

My mother sucked her teeth and turned her attention back to her beer. I kept my mouth shut and made my way back to my room to check on Tahjae and Iyana. Grabbing my jacket, I made my way to leave the house. At seventeen, with a child, I felt like my mother didn't need to be in my business. Of course, I went along with it to stay in her good graces.

When I made it downstairs, the building door slammed behind me. Rocky was already sitting on the benches waiting on me. I've had quite a few friends, but I connected best with Rocky. She didn't judge me. Since I had given birth to Iyana, I had gained some weight and I wasn't feeling like myself. It looked good 'cause it was in the right places but I couldn't shake the feeling of being fat. I was 5'7" and last I checked, I was two hundred and thirtytwo pounds. I wore most of the weight in my hips, thighs, and titties. My breasts both together had to weigh at least eight pounds each. They went from a Ccup to a tripleD in a matter of months while I was pregnant with Iyana. They just never went back down. From then on, I had constant back pain, pain that was sent from the devil himself.

"Rocky! What's up, girl?" I said ecstatically.

"Shit, nothing. I got cold waiting for your ass to come down."

"Oh, stop!" I chuckled. I pulled out a prerolled blunt and sparked it. Rocky didn't smoke, so I was going to enjoy this facial.

"I'm serious. What took you so long?"

Sighing, I began to tell Rocky about my mother stopping me and the bad news of Raheem not being Iyana's father. I expressed to Rocky how fucked up I was behind it 'cause I allowed one night of lust to come in between us.

"So, what are you going to do?" Rocky asked, still flabbergasted.

"Tell her real father that he's a daddy."

"And who might that be? Do I know him?"

Laughing, I responded, "Girl, everybody in Red Hook knows him."

Rocky twisted up her face. Her face showed that she was trying to figure out who he could be. When she looked at me, I adverted my eyes up to Charity's window. It took a second for Rocky to catch on but when she got it, her bottom lip dropped and she appeared to be blown away by the news.

"Bitch! What? When? How?" she exaggerated.

"Would you keep your voice down? It was only one time."

"You know he fuck with Ni'Shea right?"

"Yeah, I know. But I didn't know that he was at the time. It definitely would have changed the dynamics and he wouldn't even have been able to sniff the pussy."

Rocky spat there stunned, trying to piece together everything. She asked, "So what are you going to do?"

"Tell him, like I said. Just because he with Ni'Shea don't mean that he can't know that Iyana is his. I'd rather get this shit done now while she's little than wait 'til later on."

"When you gonna tell him?"

High as hell, I clipped my blunt against the gate and responded, "Well, I was going to wait until tomorrow so my mother could be there with me, but fuck it. I'm here right now. Might as well. You coming?"

"Bitch, you crazy. I'll wait for you right here."

Laughing, I shook my head and walked inside of Charity's building. I walked up the stairs and reflected back to almost a year ago. Charity had seen me outside one day and she was playing with Iyana. She asked me if I was sure that Iyana wasn't her brother baby. At the time I was sure, but now as I walked up the stairs, my heart thundered in my chest as I wondered what the fuck was going to happen. I took a deep breath and knocked on the door, holding my breath until someone came and opened the door.

"Who is it?" I heard Jaquan's voice boom through the door.

"Korrin," I said loud enough for him. But I doubt that he did with all of the background noise that was going on in the apartment.

The locks on the door came undone and Jaquan appeared. He stepped out of the apartment and into the hallway. He was just in black jeans, the tops of his boxers showed, and half of his hair was undone from the cornrows he rocks.

"What's up, Korrin?" he asked and smiled, showing his perfectly white teeth.

Damn, was he always this damn fine before? I couldn't help but to think. His brown skin looked like it was laid on his bone structure by God himself. His brown eyes twinkled under the lighting from the florescent bulbs and his abs screamed out at me.

"What up? You got a minute to talk?"

"Yeah."

Inhaling and getting a grip over my nerves, I said, "So I don't know any other way to tell you than to tell you. My daughter is yours."

There was a pregnant pause before he responded, "Are you sure?"

"Yes, I am. I was fucking with somebody else when I fucked around and had sex with you. I got a DNA test results saying that he isn't the father. So that leaves you. We could do a DNA test if you want to."

"Of course. If she mine, I'll take care of her. You don't have to worry about that. What you about to go do though? You gonna be around so we could talk about it some more?"

"Yeah. I'm just gonna be right downstairs with Rocky."

"A'ight, give me a second and I'll be down."

I nodded my head and made my way back downstairs. A weight was lifted off my shoulders and I felt like everything was going to be alright. Rocky was waiting for me on the bench and jumped up when she saw me approaching. Questions flew from her mouth before I even got close to her.

"What happened? Was he mad? Is he gonna step up and be a father?"

I laughed and responded, "Everything is all good, and no he wasn't."

"Korrin! You said my brother is Iyana's daddy!" I heard loud mouth Charity say. She had come downstairs with a big-ass KoolAid smile on her face.

"Yes."

"Didn't I tell you she looked like him? I kept asking you and you kept telling me no. I knew it!"

While we were laughing, there was ruckus going on in the hallway. Jaquan and Ni'Shea came bursting out of the door. I didn't know that she was there. I would have waited until he was alone.

"You said Jaquan was the father of your baby!" she yelled. Jaquan had positioned himself between us.

"Yes." My high now blown.

"What do you mean? Like how?" Jaquan asked. I was confused as shit because not even five minutes ago he was talking about he'd take care of her.

"What do you mean how, Jaquan? Add it up. The time y'all had sex and the nine months that she was pregnant, dummy," Charity stated, twisting up her face, causing me to laugh.

Ni'Shea and Jaquan were going back and forth arguing. She was talking shit towards me, but I let that shit roll off my back. Had I known that they were together, I wouldn't have had sex with him, I wouldn't even have entertained him. She needed to keep on checking him and stop running her dick suckers at me. The fiasco was done as quickly as they had come downstairs. Charity was the happiest of the trio as she made her exit after the arguing, loving couple made it upstairs.

What did I get myself into? Once they went upstairs, I called it a night and went home. My mother was starting her shit as soon as I got inside the house. This wasn't how I wanted the rest of my life to be. Something was going to give, but I didn't know it was going to take years and two more kids to happen.

Six weeks later and the DNA test results had come back. I had gotten my letter first and it was 99.9% that she was Jaquan's daughter. I relished that moment and let it stew in my mother. She didn't have anything against Jaquan and his family, but Charity was messy at times and she didn't want any parts in that.

He kept to his word and did what he had to do for Iyana at least he did, until I moved upstate.

Mimi

Chapter Four

2015

Oohoo child things are gonna get easier
Oohoo child things'll get brighter
Someday, yeah
We'll get it together and we'll get it all done.

"I don't like the way these pants fit," I spoke to my best friend Keesha, who was sitting on my bed. We were getting ready to go out for the night and I couldn't find anything that would fit me good. I was on my fourth outfit change, in faded blue jeans with a white blouse tucked in, black Michael Kors belt with the gold buckle, and my strappy gold open toe Steven Madden heels.

"Girl, you look fine. By the time we get to where we going, they gonna be closing."

"Bitch, shut up. It's only ten," I responded looking at the time on my phone. This was my first weekend in a long time that I was kidsfree. In 2009, I had to leave New York City. My youngest son, Julian, his father was doing dumb shit. He was smoking dust and broke into our neighbor's apartment and someone saw him do it. You would have thought that she would have called the cops, but she didn't. Instead, she called CPS on us. Told them people that we were doing drugs and all types of crazy shit. We were tested and while I passed, he failed. The amount of PCP that they found in his system was very high. My CPS worker stated that PCP was a hallucinogenic drug and being in that environment wasn't good for my kids. She gave me two options. One, I could move back home with my mother, or two, they could take my kids. Obviously, I chose the latter. I did them one better and packed up myself,

Iyana, Matthew, and Julian, and moved upstate. Tahjae and Thomasina were there so I knew I wouldn't be by myself.

"A'ight, let me change one more time." There was this black spaghetti strap, asymmetric dress hanging in my closet that I had forgotten about. When I put it on, it fit my body just right, like the way I needed it to. I kept on my gold strappy shoes and placed gold hoops in my ears. I ran a comb through my bob, and gave myself a quick look in the mirror. Finally I was satisfied with my look and I was ready to go.Since I had moved upstate New York, things had begun to get better. I was able to complete my GED and I was currently going to school for my bachelor's in forensic psychology. It was super hard for me, but I had to do what any single parent would do. I needed to make something of myself for the sake of my children. Their fathers were deadbeats and I had no choice but to do this thing on my own. This night, for me, was much needed, and my best bitch Keesha was going to make that I enjoyed myself for the whole weekend. After everything that happened when Iyana was born, Thomasina eventually started to come around, and now she always wanted to have the kids over. Julian was the same age as her last son, which she ended up having once she had gotten settled when she moved.

"Should I call the cab now?" Keesha asked, rolling her eyes.

"Listen here, bitch. I ain't going to be taking too much more of your attitude. You know this is my first time stepping out in forever. I want to make sure that I look perfect. I'm trying to snag me a baby daddy or two." I giggled.

"Yeah, yeah, yeah. Girl, you would think that you would be over dealing with baby mama drama after your last situationship."

Now it was my turn to roll my eyes. I didn't need a reminder. Pouring myself a shot of Patron Silver, I threw it back.

The liquor burned my throat and chest and the face that I made said I didn't like it at all. Finally, I responded, "Girl, do not remind me. My comment was a joke. I vowed to not fuck with another nigga with kids and I am sticking with it."

His name was Tremaine. I met him a few years after I had moved upstate. He was the first dude that I had taken seriously. We were together for ten months when shit hit the fan. One night, after I had sent the kids to bed, I had him over. He hadn't met my children yet, nor did he know I had any. The question never came up and I never disclosed it. Choosing to keep that part of me hidden was due to failed relationships. Previously, they would interact with my children and then ghosted once we were done. I didn't need that no more. My kids' feelings mattered to me and I had to protect them at all costs.

The clock was slowly hitting eleven and Kevin Hart's standup comedy special was coming to an end. There was a knock on the door. I wasn't expecting anyone, so I figured that I wouldn't answer it. The knocking slowly turned to into banging and the only thing I could think was that this was one of my family members and it was an emergency. On top of that, the kids were sleeping and had school in the morning. The banging needed to stop. Getting up, I went to my door and opened it. On the other side of the door was a woman. Besides the apparent anger on her face, she was beautiful. Her skin was the color of toffee and flawless. Not a blemish in sight. She was dressed in grey sweat pants, a loosefitting Tshirt, boots, and a scarf. A look of confusion etched across my face because I didn't recognize her.

"Yes, can I help you?" I asked.

"I know Tremaine is here. His car is sitting outside. Let him out or both y'all asses getting beat," she said. Her expression was flat, and she was waving her fingers in a "come on" motion.

"I'm sorry, I don't know what you are talking about. How do you know Tremaine?"

"Tremaine is my nigga, bitch. I've come to collect him."

Turning to the couch, I looked at Tremaine, who was sitting on the couch acting like he didn't even hear shit that was going on. Who the fuck is this chick? I thought to myself.

"I think there may be some – um – confusion."

"Bitch, there ain't no confusion. We got four kids together and been through too much shit for him to think he could be out here doing whatever the fuck he wants. Now this my last time, bitch, tell him to get his shit"

"I'm not about to be any more bitches! You need to pipe that shit down and remember, you came knocking on my door. I didn't come to you."

"Bitch, do it look like I give a fuck about your damn house? I said what the fuck I said."

This bitch was pushing my buttons, but I kept my cool for the sake of my kids. Turning my attention to Tremaine, I said, "You want to explain this? Why is she knocking on my door? Y'all together?"

"Man…I don't even know what she is talking about," Tremaine responded.

"Oh, you don't know what I'm talking about, Tremaine?" she yelled. I looked towards my kids' room to make sure that they hadn't woken up.

"You gonna have to lower your voice," I stated calmly.

"And you need to move so we could handle this before you find your ass getting dragged!"

Tremaine jumped from the couch, placing his shoes on his feet. He said, "Linda, go your ass home. You know good and damn well we not together! You are doing the fucking most!"

"I'm not gonna say shit to y'all again! Shut the fuck up with all this yelling!"

Bitch, what the fuck you gonna do about it?"

At my wit's end, I balled my fists and before I was able to swing, Linda charged at me. She swung at my face, but I was quick enough to move out of the way. She was now in my home, so I had all rights to defend myself. Yanking her by her shirt, I punched her in the mouth, opening her lip up. Right there in the living room, we were brawling. I give it to her, even though she was losing, she put up a fight. She fell to the floor and I got on top of her, airing her shit out.

"Korrin, get off her!" Tremaine yelled while pulling on my shirt. No matter what he was doing, I wasn't letting up.

"Ma!" That was my youngest son, Julian, calling my name. That was when I stopped. Tremaine's baby mother was bleeding from her face, but still trying to put up a weak fight. I got off her and noticed all three of my children were standing in the kitchen doorway.

"Bitch, you got kids?" Tremaine asked in shock.

"Get your shit and your baby mother off my floor and get out of my house," I said trying to catch my breath.

Tremaine shook his head and proceeded to get his baby mother from off the floor, all the while cursing her out. That was the last time I'd seen both and vowed that the next dude I was to take seriously had to not have children. I was good with the baby mama drama.

Beep! Beeeeep! Beeep!

Bringing me back to reality was the cab honking outside my door impatiently. Both Keesha and I took two extra shots each and stumbled out of the house to get in the cab. Rethinking about the old situation with Tremaine had put me in a slightly bad mood. I promised as the house door closed behind me to have a good time.

Mimi

Chapter Five

It's Friday night and the weekend's here
I need to unwind, where's the party, Mr. DJ?
I am ready to call my friends
So we could all get down

By the time Keesha and I made it to GVO Hookah Lounge, the place was almost packed. After having out I.D's checked, we made our way to the bar and ordered tequila shots. After our shots, we ordered tequila sunrises and found us a seat at a table that was off to the corner to peep what was going on. The DJ decided to throw on "Drop It Low" by Ester Dean and I began to sit in my seat.

"No ma'am, you said that you wanted to have fun, so grab your drink and let's hit the dance floor," Keesha stated as she pulled me from my seat.

"But I don't want to lose our seats." I pouted.

"Bitch, let's go!"

Shaking my head, I chuckled and followed her onto the dance floor. My booty had a mind of its own as it bounced to the beat. Keesha was off to the side, hyping me as usual. "Drop It Low" went off and the DJ threw on "Never Leave You" by Lumidee. Keesha made sure that I never sat down for the remainder of the night. Our plan was to only stay until one, but we ended up leaving at three when the lounge closed. There was a slight crowd hanging around the entrance of the lounge and it seemed like, no matter how many times we said "excuse me", nobody was moving. Doing what any other drunk person would do, we pushed our way through.

"Watch where the fuck you going!" a female yelled and pushed me, causing me to stumble over a crack in the ground."

"Bitch, who the fuck you think you pushing?" Keesha said, turning around to face the girl.

"Y'all just bum rushing through everybody like y'all don't see everybody standing around."

"Bitch, we said excuse me. If you ain't move, that ain't on us. Put your hands on me one more good time and being pushed will be the least of your worries," I interjected. She was lucky to catch me when I wasn't paying attention. That stumble sobered me up some and I was now on point.

"Bitch? Who you calling a bitch?" she questioned, walking up to me with her arms folded. Two other girls followed behind her.

"The dog that's magically standing on her back legs in front of me."

Security saw that the situation was getting heavy, so they stepped in between us. The tallest of the two said, "Okay, ladies, let's call it a night. It's late and the fun is over."

Keesha and I stared down the girl and decided to be the bigger women and turn to walk away. The ringleader cackled and said, "Yeah, I fucking thought so."

Keesha and I paused in our movements and looked at each other. Keesha turned around and walked up to the girl. She yelled, "Bitch, I don't know who the fuck you think you talking to, but you need to check yourself. And while you at it, get some clothes that fit you cause your titties over there trying to pop the fuck out of your top, wanting to say hi to me."

Laughter erupted as Keesha read this poor woman to filth. Even her friends were laughing at her. The look on her face read embarrassment and she tried to lunge at Keesha. The security guard jumped in between the two, catching the girl by her waist. To be extra petty, I stuck my tongue out and skipped away. Grabbing a cab, Keesha and I laughed all the way back to my house.

***

Rays from the sun beamed down on my face from the window. I don't know why I chose to have sheer curtains. I hated when the sun woke me up. Stretching my limbs, I leaned onto my elbows and looked down at myself. I still had on the dress from the night before and my breath was funky times a hundred. I climbed out of the bed and walked into the bathroom. On my way there, I peeked into the kids' rooms to check on Keesha. My heart dropped to my ass when I noticed that she was gone, and I tried to remember if she had come home with me. I made my way into the living room and saw her passed out on the floor with the air conditioner blasting and wrapped in a blanket.

"Keesha. Keesha! Get your ass up off the floor." I chuckled. My voice was a tad bit hoarse and I stumbled a bit.

Keesha stirred around on the floor before she rolled over onto her back. "Damn, Korrin, what you want?" she asked with her eyes still closed.

"Get up, you on the floor."

"Don't be annoying."

"Fine, bitch. I'm trying to help your ass out. I'm going to shower and get us some breakfast. Be off the floor by the time I get back."

Shaking my head, I got up from the couch and made my way to the bathroom. My hair was a mess. Instead of doing something to it, I just brushed it down and put my scarf over it and climbed into the shower. Twenty minutes later and with my body clean from the previous night activities, I went to my room to get dressed.

Keesha found her way into my room, where she was comfortably leaning against my pillows, stuffing her face with Oreos.

"You are worse than the kids. I told you that I was going to get breakfast."

"I couldn't wait. My stomach would have dropped to my feet if I would have continued to wait."

Rolling my eyes, I dried off with a towel and proceeded to get dressed. Keesha was like my oldest child. She'd have me yelling and screaming as if she was part of the crew. Once I was dressed, I grabbed some money and my phone and made my way to the diner that was located around the corner.

"Make sure you bring back some coffee!" Keesha yelled as I closed the door. She may have been a handful like the kids, but I couldn't help but to love her.

"What can I get for you today, Korrin?" Ashley, the waitress, asked me.

"Just two of my usual's and two cups of coffee," I responded. I'd been coming to that diner since I had gotten my crib a few years ago. It was the only spot that served my favorite breakfast of bacon, scrambled eggs with cheese, home fries with onions and peppers, and toast like they do in Brooklyn. At that point, I didn't even know why Ashley would ask me what I wanted because that meal was the only one that I was committed to. After she placed my order, I took out my phone to get my morning dose of Facebook drama.

Five minutes later, the door dinged as someone came inside of the establishment. The smell engulfed me and was quite familiar. It was Versace Eros and my favorite smell on a man. As much as I wanted to see who the scent was coming off, I kept my face in my phone.

"Hello sir, what can I get for you today?" Ashley asked, more chipper than what she usually is.

"Do you have a menu that I could look at?" he asked. The deepness of his voice boomed and made my body shake. I've never heard a guy's voice so deep. I thought this goodsmelling man was God himself. From the corner of my eye, I noticed Ashley place a menu into his hands and walk away. His smell was intoxicating, and it was eating me up inside to want to look at him.

"Excuse me," I heard him say. I didn't pay it any mind 'cause I just knew he was calling for Ashley and not talking to me. He said it again and proceeded to tap me on the shoulder.

"Yes?" I answered and made eye contact.

"I'm new to the area and this is my first time eating here. Is there something that you recommend?"

His teeth...my God, his teeth were perfect. His green eyes penetrated mine as he asked me that question. His light brown skin laid perfectly over his bone structure. There was a scar over his left eyebrow that had cut off the end of it. The goatee that surrounded his perfect, medium full lips was lined to perfection. He was tall and muscular not overly muscular like how niggas were now a days. He was just right for his height.

"Oh, um, I only get one thing from here, so I don't think that I would be of much help," I finally said after I caught myself wrapped up in this man.

"What might that be? If you don't mind me asking."

"Bacon, scrambled eggs, home fries, and toast."

He smiled, flashing his teeth again and said, "You know what? That doesn't sound too bad. You get onions and peppers in your home fries?"

"Oh yeah. That's the only way to eat them." I giggled.

"My name is Sheek," he said. I couldn't get enough of his smile. It's like he wouldn't stop because he knew what it was doing to me.

"Korrin. Nice to meet you."

"I could say the same. Do you live around here?"

"Yes, I do, actually. Right around the corner."

Ashley came back to the bar style corner and asked, "Are you ready to order, sir?"

"Yes. I will take what she is having."

Ashley smiled and responded, "You got it. Your order is gonna be ready in five minutes."

Sheek turned around on the bar seat to face the door and asked, "How does Joe make yours?"

"Extra everything." I chuckled.

Ashley place my food on the counter with the two cups of coffee on a cardboard tray. Sheek's eyes ballooned inside his head. He said, "Oh, I don't need that much extra."

Confused, I looked between Sheek and the food. I said, "Ooh, no. My best friend is at my house eating Oreos at this very moment. I mean, I'm a girl who likes to eat, but this would be too much. And speaking of, let me get back before she eats all of my kids' sna"

I snapped my mouth shut as I realized that I mentioned my kids. I awkwardly smiled and made my way to the door. I almost made it to the corner of the building when I heard Sheek calling my name.

"Yes?" I answered.

"Let me give you my number. I could use a new friend in the area. What are you doing later on today?"

"I have studying to do."

"Ooh, you're in school."

Finding myself giggling again, I said, "I am."

"Let me give you my number and if you have a few minutes later, you could tell me about it." Sheek licked his lips and smiled that smile yet again.

"I'll give it some thought. I have an exam Monday and I need to pass this class," I mentioned, slightly lying. I slipped and said something about having kids and at that moment I wished that I could take it back.

"You okay?"

"Yeah. I just gotta get back before the food starts to get cold."

"Okay, beautiful. I hope to hear from you soon." Sheek placed my phone in my back pocket, causing me to deeply inhale his scent. Sheek winked at me and made his way back to the diner.

Rushing home, my mind flashed his pretty damn face in stages. Keesha was sitting on the couch watching TV when I entered the house. Walking into the kitchen, I placed the food and coffee onto the table. My cheeks were hurting from smiling so damn hard. Keesha came inside of the kitchen to grab her food and coffee.

"What the fuck is that on your face?" she asked.

Instinctively, my hand went to my face and I said, "What?"

"You're smiling. What the fuck happened when you went to the damn diner?"

"Nothing, skank. Today is just a good day."

Keesha eyed me and twisted up her lips. She said, "Hmph. I think otherwise. I'm gonna take this food and go home. I'll holla at you later, bitch."

My mouth dropped as she turned and sashayed away out of the door. I couldn't even be mad with her. This was Keesha and that's what she does. The high that I was on made me throw caution to the wind and I began to clean. The kids would be home in a day and I wanted to make sure that things were in order when they arrived.

Chapter Six

Then

Every thought is a battle
Every breath us a war
And I don't think
I'm winning any more
Anon

Some days are good for me and other days are bad. In 2013, I was at my lowest ever. I remember things so vividly and wish that I could turn back the hands of time. Julian's dad was mad because he didn't hold up his part of the agreement about seeing Julian, which resulted in him not being able to see him. He was supposed to stay clean from PCP and get his shit together. But he didn't. He ended up going to jail for a few months. When he got out, things turned into a shit show.

I wasn't working, and I was relying on government assistance to take care of my household. At the time, I didn't know that I was suffering from depression. While the kids were in school, I would stay in bed all day, whether I was sleeping or not. It didn't matter, my bed was my sanctuary. Soon enough old clothes, food, garbage, and everything else began to clutter my house. I didn't want anyone over. I hid from the outside world, and played like everything was everything. To me, it became my new normal. My kids were young, but I knew they felt the drastic change.

The day my life changed forever and I was forced to seek help was the worst day of my life. The kids had a half of day and we were chilling watching TV and, in my head, I was convincing myself that I was going to clean up. That never happened. Someone rang my doorbell and I initially wasn't going to answer because I hated when people would just pop up.

"Mommy, someone is ringing the doorbell," Matthew said.

"Yes, I know," I responded and walked over the junk that littered the floor and looked out of the window.

Below was a white male and female looking up at my window. I knew that I had fucked up and had no choice but to let them in. Upon their entrance, they asked me a few questions and told me that they had received a phone call saying that I was abusing my kids. My mind automatically went to Julian's father. This wouldn't have been his firsttime calling CPS on me. He has done it before, but I wasn't in the fuckedup predicament that I was now in. The female told me that I should call a relative to come and get my kids. With everything in me I wanted to cry because I knew what was coming next. Korrin, you put yourself in this position. Put on your big girl panties on and handle this, I could remember thinking. Calling Tahjae, I briefly told her what was going on and she was at my house ten minutes flat. Hugging my kids felt like it was going to be the last time. Tahjae made sure that she told me that the kids would be good.

When they left, I leaned against the wall and looked at the CPS worker. She had a look on her face and said, "Are you okay? Do you have any mental health issues?"

I sniffled as I looked at her like she was crazy. Why would she ask me such a question like that? Mental health issues? I responded and said, "No. Not that I'm aware of."

"In cases that I have seen like yours, hoarding is usually connected to mental health issues and I would like for you to see a therapist. Would you be open to that?"

A therapist? Now why the fuck would I do such a thing like that? I thought to myself. But I knew I had to agree, so I did. At that point, I just wanted to get the visit over with.

"Give me a second. I have to make this phone call," the worker said and stepped into the hall.

I sat on the couch and looked around at my apartment. I finally saw what everyone else saw and I was truly disgusted with myself. How could I let it get this far? I asked myself. I couldn't even begin to know why or how this started. My tears wouldn't stop flowing and my mind raced as I tried to figure out what was going to happen next. Hearing the door open, I looked up and the CPS worker was making her way back inside of the apartment, but this time she wasn't alone. Troy Police Department was with her and my heart dropped to the pits of my stomach.

"Korrin, this is just procedure. Your kids are safe with your sister and we will be following up," she stated.

The officer looked at me and reached behind him to take his cuffs out and headed in my direction. Standing from the couch, my head spun as the cuffs were tightened around my wrists and I was taken down to the squad car.

Now….

The sun beamed down on me through the trees as I came back to reality. My life thus far had been one for the books, but I was determined to keep moving for the sake of my kids. Looking down at my phone, I realized that I still had an hour before I was to make my way from the park back to my house to wait for the kids.

The weather was beautiful, and I intended on soaking every last bit of it until it was time for me to go. Studying needed to be done and I needed to stop thinking about my past.

I opened my books up yet again and began to take notes when someone's shadow covered my book. Instantly, I became annoyed and looked up, fully prepared to curse out whoever it was who had the audacity to block my sunlight. My words swam around my mouth when I realized who it was.

"Am I blocking the sun?" Sheek asked with a smile on his face. He stood in front of me with grey basketball shorts, a beater, a durag, with Jordans on his feet. Sweat was dripping from his forehead and his beater was damp.

With a smile on my face, I responded, "Yeah, just a little bit."

"My bad. Hello, Miss Korrin."

"Hey yourself."

Sheek sat down next to me on the grass and peeked at me. There was a brief pause both of us probably wondering what to say. Then, awkwardly, we both began to talk. I let him go first.

"I don't know what it is about you, but you make me speechless. I'm usually a talkative person but I have absolutely nothing to say."

"Something about me?" I asked, placing my hand on my chest, acting like I was flabbergasted.

"Yes, you. Something is telling me that I need to get to know you. What are you doing in the park alone?"

"I like to come here and study. I try to get here as much as I can to get peace of mind."

"I can dig it. For the most part, it is quiet. A couple of dudes I know bailed on me and I'm glad that they did. I probably would have missed you."

Closing my book, I decided to give Sheek my time for the next hour. He was an intriguing person and could hold an impressive conversation.

I was caught up in our conversation and was late making it back home. He offered me a ride to my house, and I couldn't help but to protest. I couldn't let my kids see me being dropped off by some random. That was not the move. As pressed as I was about not letting him take me home, he made a valid point and said that he wouldn't feel right if he let me walk home by myself, and it was beginning to get dark. After five minutes of convincing me, I gave in. My house was only a fiveminute drive and Thomasina had the key. The kids will be in the house anyway, I convinced myself.

The ride was quiet partly because I was praying that everybody was in the house when I got there. Luckily for me, they were. I thanked Sheek and climbed out of the car and bolted to the door.

"Korrin!" Sheek called my name.

I paused at the door and turned to give him my attention. "Yes?"

"Let me take you out. We could do whatever it is you want to do."

"It sounds fun. I'll give you a call later in the week and we could set something up then."

Sheek smiled his perfect smile and responded, "I'm giving you until Wednesday. If I don't get a phone call, I'm calling you."

"But you don't have my number."

"Yes, I do. I called myself before I gave you your phone back. I knew from the jump that you were a tough cookie to crack, but I was determined to do everything to get to know you."

A smile crept onto my face and I couldn't help but blush. I watched Sheek turn his back and make his way back to his car. The smirk on my face lasted all of two seconds because the door to my apartment swung open and Keesha was standing there with her hands on her hips.

"Where have you been?" she asked while tapping her foot.

"I was at the park studying. Where are the kids?"

"Watching a movie in your room."

Walking into the house, I put my books down on the table and went to go greet the kids. While they had a good time at their aunt's house, they were happy to be home with me. Leaving them to finish the movie, I went into the kitchen to start dinner.

"What are you doing here?" I asked Keesha, who was sitting on the counter.

"Sunday dinner, duh."

Rolling my eyes, I responded, "Keesha you here every fucking day for dinner. I honestly don't know why you have food in your house."

"When I'm not here, I do eat at home, heifer."

Keesha was my best friend and of course, I didn't mind her eating at my house, but she was gonna do me a favor this time. After I placed the water on the stove for mac and cheese, I turned my attention to Keesha and said, "Are you doing anything this weekend?"

"Nothing that I could think of. Why? What's up? You want to go back to the Hookah Lounge?" she asked.

"Not exactly. Remember the dude that I told you I met at Lorenzo's?"

"Yeah, what about him?"

"I ran into him while at the park today and he wants to take me out."

Keesha looked at me up and down with a smirk on her face and said, "Oh, so you trying to get some dick, huh?"

"Bitch. No. I just think that it's time for me to start to get to know someone. I'm always with the kids and focusing on school that I think that I should focus partly on a little play thing for a while. You know that I'm kind of skeptical of being in something serious. I just want to have fun."

"Girl, you don't have to explain nothing. You know I'm all for you being happy. You know my godkids are in good hands. We gonna have fun all weekend."

"No, no, no. I'm not leaving for the whole weekend. I just need you to watch them one night. Either Friday or Saturday."

"Girl, I got you."

"You're a life saver. I don't know what I would do without you."

"That's what family is for. I'm pretty sure that if I had kids, you would do the same thing."

"I'm glad you realize that. Now start chopping onions and peppers," I said with a smirk.

Mimi

Chapter Seven

Ain't nobody worried 'bout no money
And we still gonna have a good time
Like JJ, Thelma, and Willona, we gonna have a good time

Saturday was here, and I was excited to be going out with Sheek. I'd been busy with school, but Sheek made sure that he texted me every day since we had seen each other at the park. Every morning when I woke up, there was a "good morning beautiful" text. Already, I felt like this was too good to be true. Keesha was at my house as usual, helping me get ready. Iyana sat on my bed, watching me frantically throw clothes all over my room.

"Korrin, you are thinking way too much into this," Keesha stated.

"This is my first date in I don't know how long. I have to look perfect."

"Mom, whatever you decide to wear, you will look beautiful anyway," Iyana butted in.

"Thank you, baby, but you don't understand the pressure of looking perfect for the first date."

"Did he say what y'all were doing? That way, you could know what to wear," Keesha asked.

"No. For all I know, we could be going to a ball or going to Grafton." I sat down on my bed, feeling defeated. I'd never had this much stress over my life.

"Text him and see if he would let you know where y'all going."

"It's no use because I've tried to all week to get a clue. He won't tell me shit."

Getting back up and heading to my closet once again, I decided that I'd just wear a simple white ruffled baby doll dress that stopped at my knees and flowed at my wrists. I paired that with brown wedges and my brown and white Michael Kors crossbody bag. My hair was freshly done in long black and red kinky twists, styled into a bun.

"How do I look?" I asked, checking myself out in my full body mirror.

"Bomb, bitch! Yasss!" Keesha exclaimed and I couldn't help but to smile. If I had to admit to myself, I did look damn good.

"I'm nervous as shit though."

"Don't be. Just be yourself and everything will fall into place."

As I was putting on the last bit of accessories to make my outfit pop, the doorbell rang, and my armpits began to sweat. Both Keesha and Iyana ran to the door to be nosy.

"Iyana!" I called behind her. I didn't want him to meet any of my children yet and here her nosy ass was ruining that plan. Calming myself down, I heard Keesha invite Sheek in and let him know that I was just doing some finishing touches and she would come and get me. My hands were on my hips when Keesha and Iyana walked back into my room, giggling.

"Keesha, I'm get your ass later. Iyana, stay in a child's place and mind your business. When you hear me call you, you bring your ass back, do you understand me?" I spoke sternly.

"Yes ma'am."

"Keesha, don't have them tearing up my damn house. I'll try to be back by ten."

"Girl, go and have fun. If you happen to stay out, then so be it. The kids are good. Now go. You got that man out there waiting for you."

Rolling my eyes, I got my nerves together and walked out of the rook. Sheek was looking at the family photos on the wall. The smell of Versace Eros emitted from his body and he looked delicious wearing faded blue jeans, a light blue Vneck polo shirt and white Nike high top Air Force One's.

"Ahem," I said, announcing my arrival.

Sheek turned around with a bouquet of pink carnations, white button spray chrysanthemums in a pink ceramic vase. They were the most beautiful flowers I'd ever seen and I couldn't help but to look at them in awe.

"Wow, you look beautiful. Here, these are for you," he spoke with a smile on his face.

"Thank you. They are beautiful." I took the vase away from Sheek and placed them on the dining table.

"You ready?" Sheek asked.

"Of course. Lead the way."

Sheek was pushing a different car today. It was a white 2015 Mercedes Benz class GL 550 AWD 4matic. He had left the truck running and the cold air from the air conditioner welcomed us. The seats were buttery soft, and I was thoroughly impressed already.

"You gonna tell me where we are going?" I asked.

"Nope. That would ruin the surprise. It's been a while since I've been able to surprise a woman."

"What if I don't like surprises?"

"What? Who doesn't like surprises?" Sheek asked with shock in his voice.

"A lot of people don't. Luckily for you, I'm not one of those people, but I don't like to be held in suspense."

Sheek grabbed my hand and interlocked his fingers with mine. Kissing the back of my hand, he said, "Trust me. Nothing that I have planned today is going to hurt you."

"Okay. I'll leave it alone for now." I placed my shades over my eyes.

Between the music and making small talk, I didn't realize how much time had slipped away. We pulled into a shopping outlet and parked. I looked around, wondering why we were here. Sheek climbed from the driver seat and made this way over to my side to help me out.

"What I have planned, I know that you aren't prepared for it. So, I'm going to take you to shop for what you need before we head on over to our destination," Sheek announced as I climbed out. After he made sure the doors were locked, we walked inside of the outlet and headed towards The Gap. Sheek headed over to the beachwear section and smiled at me.

"Oh, so I'm gonna need a bathing suit. Okay! Clue one," I said with a giggle.

Sheek chuckled and left me to look at the bathing suits. There weren't too many cute ones to choose from, so I chose a simple white two piece that had silver swirls designed on it. I picked up sheer white pants and white flip flops. I found Sheek waiting for me at the register with a pair of blue trunks, beach towels, a white beach hat for me, and a tan bucket hat for himself. We approached the register and placed our items on the counter. Going inside my purse I reached for my wallet, but Sheek stopped me.

"What you are reaching in your purse for?" he asked. His eyes locked with mine as a smirk appeared onto his face.

"To pay for my items," I stated, looking at him like he was crazy.

"Nah. You don't have to pay for anything. I invited you out, so it's only right that I pay."

With a wink of his eye, he turned back to the cashier, who stood there flabbergasted. She snapped out of it and began to bag our items. I was just as shocked as the cashier. It's been a while since I've never had to pay for anything, and it was refreshing.

Next up, we went to the Courtyard by Marriott Lake George. He paid for a room and we made our way to go change. The room was beautiful. There was a kingsized bed that felt like a cloud and a small desk and chair that sat under the fortytwoinch flat screen TV. The bathroom was white with marble counters and chrome accents. Finally, there was a balcony that had the most beautiful view of the lake and mountains. On the balcony was a high table with bar style chairs.

"Did you see this view?" I asked Sheek as I stood by the gate. I felt his presence behind me as he wrapped his arms around me. His head sat lightly on my shoulder and his hands were on the gate.

"It's beautiful. Just like you."

I couldn't help the smile that was on my face.

"Thank you. You're sweet. Okay, let's get ready 'cause I know we 'bout to go hit the beach." I felt the bulge in his shorts and needed to remove myself immediately before I made a decision that I would regret.

"I'll change in the bathroom, cool?"

"Yes, that's fine. Thank you for being a gentleman."

"I wouldn't be me if I wasn't. Besides, this is our firsttime chilling with each other and I want to be as respectful as I can."

"I appreciate it."

Sheek excused himself to the bathroom. Once he was inside, I called Keesha to make sure that everything was okay with the kids. Keesha went out and bought the kids a blow up pool that was four feet deep, pool accessories, and bathing suits. Before I got off the phone, she told me yet again that if I stayed out, it would be okay. With that, she hung up in my face because the pool was waiting for her.

I quickly placed my bathing suit on, took my kinky twists from the bun, and placed the hat on my head. I was checking myself out in the mirror when Sheek came from the bathroom. Just like I imagined, he was cut the fuck up with tattoos sporadically placed across his chest, arms, stomach, and back. I thanked God that his chest was hairless. It was a major turn off for me.

"Damn," I mumbled.

Sheek smiled and asked, "What was that?"

"Nothing. Are you ready?"

"Yeah, let's go."

He knew exactly what he was doing, and I knew he heard me. I promised myself to be on my best behavior.

Five minutes later, we pulled up to Million Dollar Beach. When Sheek parked the car, he grabbed a cooler and beach umbrella from the back. Oh, he was prepared, I thought to myself. The sand was soft, but hot as hell. We made it to a secluded spot and began to set up. The beach bag that Sheek was carrying was packed with a beach blanket, beach towels, and sunscreen. He set the umbrella up perfectly and made sure that it covered both of us. Once done, we took our shoes off and ran to the lake as if we were kids.

***

Four hours passed as we went back and forth from the water back to the sand. The cooler had ice cups placed in ice, pineapple Ciroc, and juice to mix. We had worked up quite a buzz so going back to the room was a major plan. We showered and headed back out to get some food from S.J. Garcia's. Sheek opted for a beef burrito and chicken enchilada while I had the serrano bacon cheeseburger. We got the food to go.

"I never asked you, only because I know that you have priorities at home. Would you be willing to stay the night with me?" Sheek asked.

We were back at the hotel. He was right, I had priorities, but I knew the kids would be good with Keesha. Why not have a night of fun? It wouldn't hurt anyone.

"I would be willing. Plus, both of us have been drinking and while I noticed that you've been handling your alcohol, going back to Schenectady is too far," I reasoned.

"Okay. Sounds good. I know that neither you nor I have any sleepwear. Let's head back to The Gap to grab something."

Nodding my head in agreement, I sent a text message to Keesha to let her know that I would be in fact staying out with Sheek. She replied with a picture of her and the kids in the pool telling me to have fun and not to come back pregnant. As a single parent, it's hard at times to let yourself have fun, especially if it's someone in my situation. I'm all my kids have and I'm always around them. Me out enjoying myself…in my mind it was wrong because they weren't with me. But that was something that I needed to learn.

Mimi

Chapter Eight

See, I told her
The devil is a liar
Them other girls can't compete with mine
You do it so, you fuck my mind

Fed and full, Sheek and I decided that it was still early enough to continue our drinking. It was going on seven o' clock and the sun was making its way to go down. Our balcony was shaded, so we decided to sit at the table and enjoy music from his phone. He had Pandora and I didn't. The view was breathtaking, and I only wished that I had this view back home.

"Is Sheek short for something? Or did you mom actually name you Sheek?" I asked.

"Actually, it's short for Shameek. My little brother couldn't pronounce it and called me Sheek. From there, it stuck."

"How many siblings do you have?"

"Three: an older sister and of course, my younger brother. I was a twin butahemshe died when we were very young."

"I'm sorry to hear that," I mentioned. He started to sound like he was getting chocked up, so I didn't bother to ask how. If he wanted to tell me, he would on his own time.

"It's all good. What about you?"

"Six. An older brother, two older sisters, one younger sister, and two younger brothers." Although we had our differences, I still claimed them. They were family at the end of the day.

"Ooh, that must have been fun growing up."

Exaggerating a laugh, I said, "Not so much. So many different personalities under one roof, how can I say? It was interesting."

"There had to be some type of fun." Sheek said with a smile.

"Don't get me wrong, there was some, but everybody grew up and kind of went their own way."

Sheek leaned over and grabbed a handful of my twists that had fallen to the front of my shoulders. He pushed them back with a smile on his face and said, "I like to see your face."

My body shuddered at his touch and I almost lost all my morals. We continued to drink and talk until the sun went down. I learned a lot about him and I enjoyed his company. We were both more than buzzed by nine and were slowly dancing to Toni Braxton singing about unbreaking her heart when Sheek placed soft kisses on my neck. Once again, my body tingled at his touch. I knew I shouldn't be allowing this, but to be honest, it'd been so long since I felt the touch of a man I craved. Sheek stood behind me and held me at the waist as he pushed his pelvis into my butt. Slowly, his hands glided up to my breasts and cupped them, softly squeezing them.

"Do you want me to stop?" he asked, whispering in my ear.

I was only able to shake my head no. In fact, I wanted him to continue. I got my wish when he turned me around and looked me in my eyes. They searched my face before I felt his hand slightly grip my neck and his mouth was on mine. It took me seconds to compute to my brain what was happening, and I shut my eyes and kissed him back.

His tongue was sweet, and his hands gripped my ass. Sheek backed me against the wall and lifted me up. My legs wrapped around his waist and my panties were damp between my legs. Little moans escaped my mouth as I grinded my waist into him.

"Sss…" I moaned as I felt his finger slide across my clit through my panties.

"Let me know if you want me to stop."

"No. I don't want you to stop."

Sheek's mouth was on mine again as he walked me over to the bed and laid me down. He was between my legs, kissing my neck and pulling my panties down at the same time. Thank God, I keep the grass cut, I thought. Once my panties were off, he sat on his knees, looking.

"You have the prettiest pussy I have ever seen," he stated with his teeth on full display.

My hands shot to my face and my legs snapped shut in embarrassment. I yelled, "Oh my God! Why would you say that?"

"Baby girl, that is a compliment. I can appreciate a pretty-looking pussy. Stop playing and open them legs again," Sheek said kissing my knees.

He pried my legs open and laid on his stomach. His lips pressed against my inner thigh, leaving a wet trail up to my moistness. His tongue flicked across my clit, causing my eyes to roll. It'd been years since I'd had this type of stimulation and it was sending me to heaven. He kept a steady pace and I was seeing Jesus himself. Apparently, I was running, and his arms wrapped around my legs to keep me in place. If only he knew how amazing it felt.

"Oh my God! Sheek! Damn," I moaned.

His tongue was working overtime on my bean and I was on the verge of leaving my wetness on his face. I was grabbing at any and everything to place in my mouth so that I could quiet myself, but there was nothing. Telling myself fuck it, I came all over his face and convulsed at the same time. Sheek left me on the bed just that way as he got up from the bed and went to the bathroom. If I smoked cigarettes, I would need one right about now, I thought while looking up at the ceiling. I couldn't help but wonder how many females he sent to see Jesus.

"You mind if I smoke?" Sheek asked as he came out of the bathroom. He was in all of his naked glory while holding a blunt to his lips.

My mouth dropped as I shook my head no. Casually, he sauntered over to the balcony and sat at the table, a cloud of weed smoke looming over his head moments later. I made my way to the balcony and stood behind him and placed kisses on his back while he smoked. I didn't smoke weed as much as I did when I was younger, but I did dabble from time to time. I took the blunt from his hand, took two long drags, and gave it back to him.

Surprising myself, I grabbed the condom from the table, that he obviously bought to use, and opened it. His dick was semihard and all it took was a kiss from my lips to get him at full attention. Coincidently, "Good Kisser" by Usher was now playing. Rolling the condom onto his dick, I made sure that it was on there nice and snug. And then I allowed him to check himself. Placing my foot on the spindle of the chair, I climbed on top of him and let his dick slide in me. Once I was comfortable, I placed my other foot on the other spindle and slowly bounced. His stare was intense as he placed the blunt in my mouth and watched me as I inhaled and tilted my head to release the smoke into the air. Sheek took another pull, placed the blunt in the ashtray, and grabbed me by the ass and assisted me in riding his dick. My hands were interlocked behind his head.

"Damn, girl," he grunted. He lifted my shirt up over my titties and pushed them together, flicking his tongue across my nipples. I was cumming on his dick and putting this pussy on him all at the same time.

Twenty minutes later, he was shooting his seeds inside of the condom and helping me down from the chair. My legs were wobbly, and I was exhausted. Making my way to the bed, I laid down and didn't realize that I'd closed my eyes until the sun was beating down on my face. Feeling skin on mine, I looked over and saw Sheek next to me naked. Immediately, I felt regret wash over my body, but even that still didn't stop the smile that was displayed on my face.

Mimi

Part 2:

During the Storm

Mimi

Chapter Nine

Always, always trust your
First gut instinct
If you feel something's wrong,
It usually is

Christmas was approaching fast, and Christmas dinner was happening at my house this year. All my siblings and my mom were going to be there, and this was the first time most of her children were going to be under the same roof. My nerves were shot because I know how my family can be. Sheek was going to be meeting my family. It was Keesha's idea, and I could have slapped myself for agreeing. My family isn't perfect, and if liquor was to get involved, it would be a disaster.

When I presented the idea to Sheek about meeting my family, I thought that he would decline. After all, Christmas was for families. Wrong! He was excited that he was going to be spending the holiday with my family. His family had flown to Arizona to see his grandmother. He sat it out due to his fear of flying.

"Besides, I can officially meet your kids. You know I love kids," was his response.

"Okay," I simply said. What could possibly go wrong?

***

Christmas Eve had arrived, and I was expecting my mom on the first thing smoking from Penn Station. Breakfast was laid out and the kids were laying around playing on the PlayStation or watching TV.

"What time is Grandma gonna be here?" Iyana asked. She always anticipated when her grandmother would come up.

"She should be here soon."

"Is she coming by herself?"

"No. Your uncles Charles, Steven, and Elijah coming up with her. Thomasina and Tahjae are gonna make their way from Troy in a few hours."

"What about Auntie Toni?"

Placing the dishrag onto the sink, I put my hand on my hip and said, "She didn't have the money for her and the kids to come. Why are you asking me all of these questions?"

Iyana shrugged her shoulders and said, "I just wanted to know who was coming. Is your boyfriend coming?"

"Girl, stay in a child's place. You will see who is coming when they get here."

"Aww, man."

"Aww, man, my ass. Get Matthew and y'all go in the closet and grab the air mattresses."

"Okay. Matt, come on! You gotta help me!"

"I don't want to!" Matthew yelled from the living room. He was in the middle of a Call of Duty match and was winning.

"Mom said so! Now let's go!"

Knowing that this wasn't going to go anywhere except for a heated argument, I interrupted and said, "Julian, help your sister. Matthew, the next time I say help and you're in the middle of a game, you're helping. And I could care less if you lose."

Matthew exhaled and said, "Yes, Mom."

Ding! Ding! Ding!

By the bell being rung, I knew it was Keesha. I opened the door and let her in. Her eyes were red and puffy, and she wasn't her happygolucky cheerful self. She smiled and tried to make it seem like she was okay. I saw right through it and sent the kids to their rooms, so we could talk.

"Kee, you good? What's wrong?" I asked, taking a seat next to her on the couch.

"I'm good, Korrin. Nothing's wrong," she said with a sniffle.

"You sure? 'Cause you don't look too good. You know you can talk to me."

"I know. I'm fine." A single tear threatened to run down her face, but she caught it.

"I'm always here for you."

Keesha dropped her head and responded, "I know. I love you for that. But it's Christmas time and I don't want to bring everyone down. When Christmas is over, I promise to tell you. Let's just enjoy family and have fun. And promise me you don't worry yourself worrying about me. I promise you, I'm fine."

"Okay. I'll leave it alone for now. You want something to eat?"

"What you make?"

I twisted my lips up and said, "I don't even know why you ask. Everything I make, you eat."

"Yeah, you right." Keesha laughed and followed me into the kitchen.

Soon enough, my family members started to show up. The adults took over the living room while the kids were sent to the room. My family gatherings were usually a hit and miss. Sometimes they went well, or they went really badly, meaning it would or could end up with somebody throwing blows.

My mom was on her fourth beer by one in the afternoon. Her bus arrived at eleven that morning and she was at my house by twelve. My house was busy with kids and adults as Keesha helped me in the kitchen with getting Christmas dinner ready. Nervously, I kept watching the time because Sheek would be arriving soon.

"Would you relax?" Keesha whispered and nudged me with her elbow.

"I can't help it," I whispered back.

"I'm sure that everyone is going to like him. Especially your mother. Y'all haven't had the best relationship, but it has gotten better since you were younger. All she wants is the best for you. Just like everyone here."

My brother Charles came inside of the kitchen, eyes sitting low and a goofy look on his face. He stood at 6'7" and towered over Keesha and me and watched us like a hawk.

"Um, Charles, what do you need? "I asked with my hand on my hip.

"I came in here to tell you something. But I forgot."

"That's cause you higher than a giraffe's pussy," I stated with a roll of eyes, which caused laughter from both Keesha and Charles.

"Korrin! You got company!" my mother yelled. My body locked because I knew it was Sheek.

"Oh yeah! That's what I was supposed to tell you. Mom said to come get you 'cause you got company."

Charles couldn't contain his laughter and I could only look at him like he was crazy. I dried my hands on paper towels and made my way to the living room. Seeing Sheek always did something to me and if my family wasn't there, I would have thrown myself on him. He turned my way and a smile appeared on his face.

"Hello, beautiful," Sheek said once I got close to him. He kissed my forehead and grabbed me into a hug.

"Hey yourself. You look and smell good, as always."

"Always for you, baby."

Tahjae, who was always on her way to being tipsy, came over to us and stopped and stood there looking. She raised one hand to her hip and said, "So you not gonna introduce your new boyfriend?"

Rolling my eyes, I said, "Girl, relax. I was finna do it, but you jumped right in on our moment."

"You know how I do. Nobody gets privacy when I'm around. Fuck you thought?" Tahjae said while flicking her hair over her shoulder.

Exhaling and trying to keep my cool, I took Sheek's coat from him and grabbed him by the hand to follow me to my room. When there, I proceeded to hang up his coat and he closed the door behind him.

"Don't mind my sister. She has had a few drinks," I mumbled.

"I'm not. I'm only worried about you and the kids. You seem just a little bit uncomfortable."

Turning to face Sheek, I wrapped my arms around his waist and looked up at him. I said, "If I'm being honest, my family is something else and liquor is playing a part, so I know this could end good or it can end bad."

Sheek chuckled. "What family doesn't have their shit with them? My family isn't perfect, and you will see when you meet them. For right now, let me go meet yours and see where it goes."

I poked my bottom lip out and looked at Sheek. He was right, but I already knew that this was going to end badly. Sheek quickly sucked my bottom lip into his mouth and smacked my ass. My clit jumped as dirty thoughts ran through my mind. When I opened my eyes, Sheek was already looking at me with a smile on his face.

"Okay, come on. Are you hungry?" I asked with my hand on the doorknob. His body was close to mine and I felt his dick on the small of my back.

"I'm always hungry for you. But I can't have you right now, so I'll wait."

A smile spread across my face and I led the way to the living room. Even the kids were in there. One by one, I introduced my family to Sheek. My brothers looked like they were trying to intimidate him, which didn't work well because they were all high, looking like giant goof balls.

"Sheek, where you from?" Tahjae asked.

"I'm from Arizona, but I've been living in New York for pretty much my entire adult life."

"And how old are you?"

"I am twentynine."

Then here comes my mother, "What do you want with my daughter? She got three kids, you think you can handle that?"

Sheek looked at me and then quickly turned his attention to my mother. He said, "Korrin and I have only been seeing each other for six months. I do see myself being with her for a long while. She's beautiful, intelligent, and knows what she wants. Her being a mother is just a bonus."

Charles stepped in and said, "Y'all leave the man alone. Korrin is grown, and if they have an understanding on what they want, that's all that matters. Yo, bro, you smoke?"

Sheek stood up and went inside his pocket. He pulled out a sack that had to be worth eighty dollars and said, "Do I?"

Charles saved Sheek from my mother's interrogation and I couldn't have been happier. While I knew it was coming from a good place, her delivery would be a tad bit overwhelming. And not to mention that Tahjae, due to the many drinks that she had, her lips were a little loose.

"Thomasina, you want to help me in the kitchen? Keesha went home to take a nap," I asked. Thomasina was the only one who wasn't drinking, and I felt she would have been a more levelheaded one to deal with in the kitchen.

"Sure. What you need me to do?" was her reply.

I explained to Thomasina what I needed her to do. All was quiet, as far as the kids playing and the adults were getting along watching TV or listening to music. I couldn't help but to think that after the rocky start, there was hope for the remainder of the day.

Looking from the kitchen, I saw Sheek getting his ass whooped by Matthew, who was enjoying giving out the ass whooping, on Call of Duty. A smile appeared on my face and was quickly wiped away when Tahjae stumbled into the kitchen. She stood next to me, drink in her hand, trying to keep her balance by leaning against the counter.

"What's up?" I asked.

"Can I talk to you for a minute? Privately?" she asked, slurring her words.

"Yeah. Meet me in my room. Let me dry my hands first," I said. She pushed herself from the counter and went towards my room. I looked at Thomasina and she shrugged her shoulders. Taking a deep breath in, I dried my hands on paper towels and made my way to my room. She was standing by the window, drink still in her hand.

"What happened?"

"You need to check your nigga," she said.

Naturally, I was surprised because I thought she was making a dramatic exit as usual. "Umm, wait, what?" I was confused.

Tahjae placed her drink down on my night stand and repeated, "You need to check your nigga. He just tried to holla at me."

I chuckled, not because I thought what she said was funny, but because I thought that what she said was absurd. I asked, "Tahjae, what makes you think that he was trying to talk to you?"

Tahjae looked at me like I had offended her. She responded, "First of all, the fact that he asked me for my number and that he said that if he wasn't with you, if he had saw me first, we would be together. He said that he loved you, but you are too fat for him. But he stays 'cause of the love he has for you."

What Tahjae said hit me in my chest like a ton of bricks. I looked at her to see if she was telling me the truth. She looked ashamed. I told her to give me a minute. I left my room and pulled Sheek away from Call of Duty to speak with him in the bathroom.

"What's up, babe? It looks like something is bothering you," he spoke. He looked at me through slitted eyes.

"I need to ask you something, and I need nothing but the truth to come out of your mouth."

"Babe, have I ever lied to you?"

He was right. He'd never told me anything to believe that it was a lie, so why would he have anything to lie about? Tahjae was my sister; why would she have anything to lie about? Before I even heard Sheek's side, I was so confused.

"Did you ask my sister for her number?" Nothing like ripping the BandAid off, right?

"No. I offered to give her mine. She was telling me about the dude that she is messing with is in jail and she was wondering if I could put him on." It was no secret between Sheek and me that off the clock he hustled. The day we were on our way back from Lake George was when he told me. What he said made sense.

"Did you tell her that if you saw her first, you'd be with her instead? That I was too fat, but you loved me so that's why you're staying?"

Sheek looked at me with anger written on his face. He gave me a long look from head to toe and when he landed on my eyes, his look softened. He took my hands into his and said, "Words like that never came from my mouth. I don't know what your sister on, but if I felt that way, I'm not the type to still be around. Fat where? You know every chance I get I'm rubbing all over your body. The whole time I was around your sister, your brothers were there. Ma, I don't know what she is talking about."

The look on his face was hard to register. I was torn in between believing my sister and my man. To most, it would be a no brainer about who to believe. It was hard for me to just choose my blood, when my blood has let me down often and has always blown things out of proportion. When I made up my mind and decided to address the issue in front of everyone, I called my brothers, Tahjae, and Sheek into the living room.

"Tahjae, can you repeat what you just told me, and I need y'all to confirm it," I said looking at my brothers. They looked confused as shit, as did Thomasina and my mother. Tahjae looked uncomfortable, and that's when I knew she was lying.

"Korrin, you doing the most," she said, waving her hand in my direction as if to dismiss me.

"Am I? 'Cause I need to know the truth." I looked between Sheek and Tahjae.

Tahjae exhaled and yelled, "Girl, don't nobody want your dude except you! You need to be checking him! He the one who was trying to give me his number!"

Charles jumped in to calm the situation. He said, "Tahjae, you making it seem like he was doing it to try to holla at you behind Korrin's back. You know what it is, and if you trying to make it seem like something other than what it is, you need to stop."

Tahjae's mouth dropped open in shock. She said, "I can't believe this shit! Y'all are always sticking up for Korrin!"

"Tahjae, that is not what this is. You've had a bit to drink and maybe you thought it was something other than what it was. It was a simple mistake," my mother interrupted.

I hated when my mother coddled her. She's been doing it all of Tahjae's whole life.

Tahjae looked at my mother like she had seven heads, like she was angered that my mother had taken up for her.

"Ain't no simple mistake. I know what the fuck just happened! Not my fault this bitch's nigga doesn't want her fat ass! It's no surprise that she wasn't gonna stick up for me! She never does!"

Here comes the Tahjae dramatics, I thought to myself. I said, "Tahjae, you need to go somewhere with your theatrics. This shit always happens, and I know that I am getting tired of it. If it ain't about you, you find a way to do so!"

"My theatrics! You need to be getting on your nigga about that shit! But yet here you are in my face, like I want anything you've had."

The room went silent until I erupted. I laughed so hard my stomach began to hurt and tears ran down my face. Getting my bearings together, I wiped my eyes and said, "Girl, it's too late for that. You done already fucked Iyana's father a few years ago."

Again the room grew quiet and all eyes darted back and forth between me and Tahjae. She looked like she was a deer caught in headlights. I found out that bit of information a few years ago. One of Tahjae's childhood friends was at her house and we were having a conversation. Drinks were involved, and she leaked the information that Tahjae had sex with

Iyana's father. At the time I didn't believe it. I thought that it was just drunk talk. I didn't care that she did it because what me and Iyana's father had was nothing. We only fucked. It was about the fact that I already had him. It's simple girl code. The next time I had heard this information was from this dude that I was fucking with from back home. He would come upstate to see me, video chat all the time, and fuck. One day we were just talking and somehow, Iyana's father came up in the conversation. That's when he dropped the bomb on me that he knew. I knew then that it was true. We'd never spoken about it before, but yet he knew.

"Don't look so surprised now," I said, kind of in a taunting manner.

"Ain't nobody had sex with your baby father!" Tahjae yelled.

"I don't even care that you did, but you out here yelling that you don't want my dude, but you have a history of sleeping with people's dudes. Let's not go down that road, Tahjae, 'cause this shit could get really messy."

Every one of my family members were silent as their eyes pinged back and forth as if they were watching a tennis match. Tahjae knew that I knew shit and she knew that I wouldn't hold back from letting shit go. She did the one thing that I knew she would do, and I was ready for that ass. Tahjae stumbled her way towards me and began yelling things in my face.

"Tahjae, you need to back up from up out of my face," I stated calmly.

"What the fuck you gonna do? You always want to dish shit out, but could never take the heat! Bitch, do something!"

"Come on now, y'all. This is getting crazy!" my mother yelled.

Calmly, I stated, "You must be out your fucking mind. This is all on you, and you always flip it around on the next person. Put the drink down and pick up the phone to call a doctor, 'cause you are seriously delusional."

"Bitch, delusional! I wish the fuck you would do something! But we all know that your fat ass won't!"

Two blows to her chest and stomach caught her off guard. Tahjae stumbled and dropped her drink and she rushed me. She went to grab my hair, but I was quicker and reached for her throat. Lifting her slightly in the air, I slammed her down on her back. Everyone gasped and decided to stop the fight. I was already on her, choking her. Charles and Sheek grabbed me to let her go. Tahjae was grabbing at my hands, the kids were yelling, and Thomasina disappeared. Sheek managed to yank me free and he began to carry me into my bedroom.

"That bitch better be out my house when I get out this room!" I yelled before Sheek slammed the door. He put me down and gave me this wild look as I placed back and forth.

"What the fuck is wrong with you! You could have killed her!" he seethed through his teeth.

"So? The bitch deserved every bit of what she got!"

"Are you stupid? That is your family!"

"That bitch accused you of trying to holla at her behind my back. Fuck is you mad about?"

Sheek's eyes grew big and he stalked over to me. He grabbed me by my arm and pushed me against the wall. The look on his face was wild and crazy. He spoke in a calm but menacing tone, "Let's get one thing straight: fuck what you got going on with your sister. You talk to me like you got some fucking sense. I'm not disrespecting you, so don't do it to me. You embarrassed me by bringing this situation to everybody and I didn't say nothing. Get yourself together and act like your fucking age and not your damn shoe size. You got your kids out there yelling and screaming. Fuck is wrong with you?"

Sheek's demeanor had changed to something that I'd never seen. My stomach turned into knots and I shook. This man standing before me I knew nothing about. It scared me shitless. I was speechless and only nodded my head. Sheek kissed my forehead and left the room.

My heart pounded in my chest and my only thought was that something wasn't right!

Mimi

Chapter Ten

Hang all the mistletoe
I'm gonna get to know you better this Christmas
And as we trim the tree
How much fun it's gonna be together this Christmas

My momma made breakfast Christmas morning. Waking up to the smell of bacon, eggs, and grits couldn't have been any better. Sheek stayed the night and his legs were wrapped around mine and his arm thrown across my waist. My stomach was growling, and it was almost time for the kids to open their gifts. I looked over at Sheek, who looked peaceful, and I wondered who the fuck he was last night.

"I can feel you looking at me," Sheek said still with his eyes closed.

"Dammit, you caught me," I said with a smile on my face.

Sheek nuzzled his face next to my neck and kissed my shoulder. "Good morning, beautiful."

"Good morning, handsome. You ready to eat?"

"Mm hmm."

"Come on," I said and proceeded to get up.

Sheek used his arm to hold me down and slithered down my body under the covers.

"What I want to eat is right here in this room," he said.

He spread my legs and climbed in between my legs. He pulled my panties to the side and his tongue circled my clit, instantly causing my kitty to drip with wetness. As much as I wanted to stop, to prevent someone from walking in on us, I allowed him to continue. He was done as soon as I came in his mouth. He came from under the covers with his face looking like a chocolate glazed donut.

"Now I'm ready," he said with a smile on his face. I grabbed my robe and went to take care of my hygiene before I joined the kids. At some point, Sheek made it to the bathroom to do the same thing.

"Good morning, y'all," I announced when I got inside of the kitchen.

Surprisingly, the kids were nowhere to be found. Everyone in the living room mumbled their good mornings back.

"How are you feeling, Korrin?" my mother asked with a mug of coffee in her hands.

"I'm fine. I'm just ready to get this day over with."

"Tahjae called me and said that she won't be coming to dinner."

"Okay. And?" I said, sideeyeing my mother.

"Maybe you should call her and apologize. I would love it
"

"I should do what? You've got to be kidding me? Why would I apologize if she was the one who was wrong?"

"To be the bigger person, Korrin."

"To be the bigger – Mama, with all due respect, she disrespected me in my house. I don't understand why you feel the need to stand up for her when she is the one who is always wrong! This is why she does what she does."

Charles jumped in and said, "Mama, Korrin is right. We get that you want things to at least be almost perfect for Christmas, but what do you expect when you are enabling Tahjae? She was dead wrong last night and she needs to be the one apologizing, not Korrin."

The kids came running from out of their rooms just in the nick of time. They ran right to the tree and began to open their gifts. My attention was quickly diverted to them and their happiness. That was the only thing that ever mattered this holiday season. Sheek finally joined us and said good morning to everybody. He and my brothers made a beeline for my bedroom to go smoke and I made my way to the kitchen for something to eat.

"Knock! Knock! Family, Merry Christmas!" Keesha yelled as she made her way inside. For a second, the kids stopped opening their gifts and ran to hug Keesha.

"Merry Christmas, Keesha," I heard my mother say.

"Merry Christmas, Ms. Samantha."

Keesha came inside of the kitchen and grabbed a slice of bacon off of my plate and chomped on it like it would be her last piece. She seemed to be in a better mood.

"I see you feeling better," I said.

"Oh yeah, a whole lot better. But what's up with you?"

"Tahjae is what's up. And like you, I don't want to talk about that right now. I will, just not today."

"Oh, then it's got to be bad."

"You already know it was."

"Okay, so to not speak about it, what's for dinner?" Keesha asked.

"Girl, it's not even nine a.m. yet and you talking about what's for dinner? Your ass always hungry. You'll see when it gets done."

Keesha twisted up her lips and began to fix her a plate of food. She paused while slapping grits onto her plate and said, "So, you're gonna starve your godchild until then?"

I dropped the plate that I was cleaning inside of the sink and looked at her. She was holding a positive pregnancy test and for the life of me, the first thought was to scream. Everybody came running in, probably thinking that I had lost my mind. I grabbed Keesha into a hug while she told me that the news of her pregnancy was my gift. It was the best gift that I could have received thus far. Maybe Christmas could turn out good after all.

Mimi

Chapter Eleven

18007997233
When you know, you know
~Korrin

January 18th was the day my life changed. I was just a few short months away from graduating and starting my job in social services. Now that things were coming down to the wire, things were becoming more stressful. The kids thought it was okay to not listen and do their chores or their homework. I needed a break and soon, soon, the kids would find a size eight up their asses. The one thing that I was grateful for was the fact that the kids were back in school from winter break. Keesha suggested that I should go away again. She offered to watch the spawns of evil, but with her being pregnant, I couldn't do that to her.

"They don't listen, Keesha. It's like since my mother left, shit has been upside down," I said, shaking my head while my phone was stuck to my face.

"That's what the problem is now. You don't whip them. They listen to me because they know I ain't afraid to grab the belt on their asses."

Changing the cycle was hard. I got my ass whooped and hated it. It was so bad that my mother allowed one of her boyfriends to whip me. But what she didn't know was that he would take joy in doing so. Alone in the bedroom, he would make me come out of every stitch of clothing, panties included, and beat me with a paddlelike stick. That's another story, for another time.

I couldn't see myself leaving the kids yet again, at least not where I was far away.

After speaking with Keesha, Sheek texted me. He said that he wanted to introduce me to his siblings. And that was when the topic of his mother came up. It never dawned on me that we'd never spoken about his mother.

"I would love to meet your siblings. I put you through the fiery pits of hell when meeting mine, I'm surprised that you are even considering that with what you had to deal with," I said when he called me that night.

"I ain't stunting on that. You could come through Friday. Oh, and can you cook too? Them loaded mashed potatoes, fried pork chops, and broccoli that I like?" I could tell that he was smiling.

"You just want my cooking."

"This new job is kicking my ass and it feels like I haven't seen you or had a good homecooked meal in forever."

"Just ask me to come cook for you. Is your mom going to be there?"

There was a pregnant pause on his end and I thought for a quick second that he hung up until he said, "No. My momma passed a few years ago. She was killed at the hands of my father. Remember when we first met, and I told you that I was fresh from prison?"

"Yes."

"That was because I beat him close to death. I don't like talking about it much 'cause it still hurts. But you are about to meet my siblings, so I don't want it to come up and you didn't know."

My heart broke for him. Granted, I didn't have the best relationship with my mother, but I couldn't imagine losing her. I'd straight up go crazy.

"I appreciate you sharing that with me. There is no need to go in depth 'cause I could only imagine the pain you feel. I will be at your house by four. I have to make sure that Keesha will watch the kids."

"Okay, babe. Let me go. I have to be at the warehouse at five and it's getting late."

My eyebrow raised. It was barely after eight and I knew how his work days could be, but something wasn't sitting right. I let it go. I told him good night and that I would see him on Friday.

***

Friday came, the eighteenth, and I was more than ready to meet his family. Climbing into an Uber, I texted Sheek to let him know that I was on my way. By the time I had gotten to his house, he still hadn't answered. On my way to his door, I called, and he answered on the third ring.

"Hey babe, I was just about to text you back. I'm still at work and I should be leaving in half an hour. The spare key is on top of the light fixture. I left it there this morning just in case I wasn't there. Be careful, it may be hot. I'll be there as soon as I can." Sheek said. The noise from the warehouse was loud as hell and I was barely able to hear him.

"Okay. I'll start dinner," I responded, and I hung up.

I retrieved the hotass key from the hiding spot and entered his apartment. I was shocked to see that nothing was out of place. When I came over, it was always miraculously clean and I thought it was because he always knew that I was coming. He knew I was coming this time, so I can't give him kudos that much, I thought. I took my snowcovered boots off at door and placed them on the rug with his boots. I hung my coat in the closet and got elbow deep in preparing dinner. He had made the pork chop thing, so I made a quick marinade for them and started on the potatoes. Fortyfive minutes later and

I was almost done with dinner. Sheek was walking inside the house with a look of tiredness on his face.

"I could get used to coming home to this," he expressed, watching me from the door. He mimicked the same exact movements that I did when I came in.

"It smells good, don't it?" I asked while dicing up the bacon and scallions for the mashed potatoes.

Sheek walked behind me and wrapped his arms around my waist and kissed my neck. He said, "Hell yeah, it smells good. I starved myself just to be able to fit every bit of it in my belly. My brother and sister gonna be here soon. Let me jump in the shower and change clothes. If they come before I'm done, don't be afraid to let them in."

Turning around, I wrapped my arms around his neck and looked at him. With a smile on my face, I watched him as he stuck his tongue out. I couldn't help but to suck on it. Just for a few seconds. I knew he would get hard and the food would burn.

"There could be more than that later on," I said and pushed him away from me.

He bit his lip and smacked my ass before he walked away. I turned back to the bacon, but before I was able to put it in the frying pan, there was a knock on the door. Taking a deep breath, I exhaled to calm my nerves and made my way to the door.

"Hi," I said once the door was open.

His brother and sister were spitting images of Sheek. His brother was just as tall as he was and rocked locs instead of the Caesar that Sheek rocked. He was dressed in jeans, Timbs, and a black North Face. His sister wore Jordan's, jeans, and a pea coat.

"Oh hey. You must be Korrin," the sister said.

"I am. Come in," I said.

"I'm Shan and this is our brother Sean," Shan said.

"What's good?" Sean said and wrapped his arms around me in a hug. It was quick, but I was a little thrown off.

"That's you in the kitchen cooking?" Shan asked, pushing Sean away from me.

"Yeah. Sheek asked me to cook."

"That's 'cause he can't cook and he knew we wouldn't eat," Sean responded, taking a seat at the kitchen table.

"Aht! Aht! Don't talk about my man. He could cook a little something something," I said with a chuckle.

Sheek came from the room with plaid pajama pants on, a white Tshirt, and slippers. He said, "That's right, baby, defend ya man."

"Nigga, get the fuck on," Sean stated.

It caused laughter between us. Dinner was done and with the help of Shan, I made the plates. We made small talk while doing so. The first five minutes everybody was chowing down and if I had to, I'd pat myself on the back because I knew Sean and Shan were enjoying it.

Shan, while licking her fingers clean, turned to me and said, "What is it that you do?"

"I'm finishing up my last year of college while I intern at Child Protective Services."

"That's impressive. What are you going to school for?"

"My bachelor's in social work. I want to be able to help children and families that truly need the assistance. There are so many people who abuse the system that when there is a family that needs the help, it's hard for them."

Sean butted in and said, "That's facts. And be the white people at that. Ain't that some shit. Last year, my homeboy had just got home from jail. He didn't want to go back to the life he was living before jail, so he went to social services for assistance. He needed help with finding a job and food stamps.

He was staying with his mom, so rent wasn't an issue. Don't you know that they flat out refused to help him? Told him to bring back documents stating that he had just been released from jail, a letter from his mom, and some other form of paperwork, just for them to even consider helping him. He brought in what he needed the next day and a month later they refused to help him. Majority of the people in that office was white and they were getting help with everything under the damn sun."

"That's how it is. When a person needs help, they either don't meet requirements by making too much or not making enough. And it's fucking sad." This was something I was truly passionate about. I vowed once I had a degree that I would do all I could to make a difference inside of my community.

"This shit is rigged by the white man to keep his foot on the black man's neck," Sean said.

"Oh my God! Here this nigga go! He 'bout to be on some shit like he Malcolm X," Shan said.

I couldn't help but laugh.

As we continued to eat, we had a debate on politics and it was hilarious. Sean spoke confidently, but he knew nothing and made no sense. When dinner was done, Shan and I sat on the couch as Sean and Sheek cleaned the kitchen. The night grew as we bullshitted around and knocked back a few drinks. It was midnight when Shan and Sean decided to leave. Sheek was way past his limit, almost passed out on the couch. I walked his brother and sister to the door.

"I really appreciate you cooking dinner tonight. It seems like you make my brother happy," Shan said.

"I hope I do. It's been a long while since I've been happy by another human, besides my kids. It hasn't been long, but it just feels like it's right."

"Be careful with him though. One day off his meds and it's downhill from there," Sean mentioned slightly with a slur. I was confused. I didn't know that he was on any medication. I asked, "What? What medication?"

Shan looked annoyed. Rolling her eyes, she said, "Bruh, you just done never know when to shut up. Don't worry about what Sean talking about. If there is something that Sheek wants you to know, he will tell you himself. Just be there for him to listen. It's not often that my brother opens up to people."

Turning their backs, Shan and Sean walked away without another word and left me looking stupid with the door open. What the fuck are they talking about? I thought.

A cold draft wafted across my feet and I hurried to close the door. I went back into the living room and looked down at Sheek, wanting to ask him what Shan and Sean were talking about. He was drunk out of his mind so I decided against it and would wait to ask another day.

Waking him up to get him inside of the room was a task in itself. He was heavy and wasn't comprehending that he needed to put one foot in front of the other to get to the room. By the time we got inside of his bedroom, I had sweat dripping from my face and on my lower back, threatening to drip to the crack of my ass.

Getting Sheek in bed was another strenuous task. I got him down to his boxers and socks and decided to grab one of his Tshirts to go shower. When I got back, my plan was to wake him up, get some of that good drunk dick, and sleep like a baby. That plan went out of the window when I walked into the room and Sheek was sitting up in bed, feet touching the floor and staring off into the distance.

"Babe?" I questioned. Slowly he turned his head in my direction and the light in his eyes was gone. There was now something dark lingering in them and it shook my body to its core.

"Where were you?" he asked in a tone that had me feeling like I was in a horror movie.

"I went to take a shower because trying to get you in bed made me sweaty," I responded.

Like a bolt of lightning, Sheek was in front of me and grabbing me by the arm. He slammed me against the wall, his face inches away from me.

"You were sweaty from laying up under another nigga, wasn't you?" he yelled.

"What? Sheek let go of me! You're hurting me! I've been with you and your siblings all night. Let go!"

"You would say anything to cover the fact that you were spreading your legs to some other nigga! Was it Doug you were fucking? Huh, Mildred? That's who it was, wasn't it! I give you a little freedom and you go and fuck the one man that I despise! Your funky ass should be home taking care of my damn kids! I got something for you!" Sheek yelled.

Did he just call me Mildred? I thought. If I wasn't sober before, I was now. I was in the middle of gathering my thoughts when I felt a stinging sensation on my face and my thoughts were now spinning around the outside of my head like stars in a cartoon. Feeling the side of my face, it was hot and swelling fast. Tears threatened to fall from my eyes, but I swallowed them. I needed to find out what was wrong with Sheek and find out how to fix it.

"Sheek, what are you talking about? I just came from out of your bathroom and was here with you the whole night. Please let me know what's going on, baby," I pleaded.

"You're a whore!" He lashed out and smacked me again, knocking me to the floor. He stood over me with a menacing look and I tried to get up, but he held me down with his foot on my chest, restricting my air flow.

Panic set in as I looked up at the man that I had fallen in love with. He was a completely different person. Fight, Korrin! My conscience yelled at me. Me fighting was the only way I was going to get the hell out of this apartment to see my kids again.

"Sheek, please get off of me!" I yelled through gasped breaths.

He listened and took his foot from off of my chest and grabbed a belt from off the wooden coat rack that he had hanging on the back of his door. I tried scooting away from him, but he grabbed me across the carpet, creating rug burn on my ass cheeks.

"You want to fuck around on me! See if I let you out of my sight again!" he yelled.

Sheek raised his arm and came down with the belt across my legs. I howled out in pain and the tears that wanted to come out when he smacked me opened up like a broken damn. He didn't stop at one. He held me by one leg and beat me across my legs, ass, and lower back with the other.

"Help! Help! Sheek, stop! Please, God, stop!" I yelled at the top of my lungs.

"If you think about leaving this house, you got another thing coming. I will sleep in front of this door if I have to, Mildred!" Sheek yelled.

"I am not Mildred!" I yelled back.

Sheek let my legs go, went to grab a chair from the kitchen, and barricaded us inside of the bedroom. I could only think about how I was going to get to my kids. Getting up from the floor was painful. I limped and cried my way onto the bed. My phone was on the dresser near Sheek and I didn't dare attempt to go get it. Sheek sat in the chair watching me with a grimace on his face.

The heat that came from his glare had me shook. I'd play his game. I moved to lay down while placing the covers over my body. Hopefully soon he would find his way to the bed and I could find my way out of this house and away from him.

**

The heavy sound of rain woke me up from a slumber that I had unknowingly slipped into. My body hurt all over as I sat up and looked around the room for Sheek. He was still sitting in the chair blocking the door. The chair was leaned back on its hind legs and his head was resting on the door. I was stuck. The tears started again because all I wanted was to see my kids again. The rain was a sign for my pain. I limped to the window to look at the sky crying for me. God worked mysteriously and there it was clear as day, something I had seen several times but completely forgotten about.

Quietly, I searched the room looking for my clothes. I found only my pants. My boots were in the living room by the door. Tiptoeing to the closet, I rummaged around and found some Jordan's, a shirt, and a coat. We weren't the same size by a long shot, but this would just have to do. Grabbing my phone from the dresser, I made my way to the window and opened it. A rush of freezing cold air entered the room. I looked over my shoulder to see if Sheek had awaken, but he was still knocked out cold.

The fire escape was a death trap with all of the ice that lined the metal structure, but I was determined to get the fuck away from Sheek and his crazy ass. Climbing through the window was an effort, but I managed. At all costs I had to go and while I was on my way down, I called for an Uber and Keesha.

"Yeah," she answered with sleep lacing her voice.

"I'm on my way back home."

"What? You could have just stayed there."

"Kee, he beat me with a belt. I couldn't. I called an Uber and I will be there shortly. Please make sure that the kids are still sleeping," I cried no longer holding in my tears.

"What?! What the fuck you mean he beat you with a belt?"

"Listen, I'll explain when I get there."

"Okay. I'll be waiting up for you. The kids should still be sleep when you get here. Just don't ring the bell. You got your key, right?"

"Shit, no! I left my purse in the living room with my boots."

"Why didn't you grab them? And if you left your boots, then what the fuck you got on your feet?"

"I couldn't get out of the room. Kee, I'm getting in the Uber now, I'll be on my way. Leave the door unlocked."

"Okay," Keesha answered and we hung up.

My body was still in a great deal of pain and the streets in Schenectady were riddled with pot holes. Every bump rocked my body with pain as if Sheek was still beating me. The ride is no longer than ten minutes, but it felt like eternity.

When I arrived home, Keesha was standing on the porch with the biggest knife I had in my kitchen. I thanked the Uber driver and made my way to her and dragged her in the house, asking why was she outside looking like a crazy woman.

"I didn't know if he followed you, so I had to be prepared," she answered.

"You're pregnant, Kee. You can't be turning up like you used to."

"Me and this baby gonna turn up behind you, fuck what you talking about."

The house was quiet except for Matthew's old man snores. We took a seat on the couch as I peeled off Sheek's coat and sneakers.

"If something happens to you or the baby, I'll go to jail. Then who would take care of my kids." I asked folding my arms to show her I meant business about her getting crazy.

"Okay, fine. But when you told me what happened, I didn't know what to do, so I made you a bath with lavender Epsom salts."

"You didn't have to do that. It's late and I already woke you from your sleep."

"Korrin, you are my most – no, scratch that you are my only best friend in the entire world, and I don't know what I would have done if I had lost you. This shit scared me half to death and drawing you a bath to soothe your aches was the least I could do. I have a lot of time to catch up with sleep. Just go relax your body and if you want to talk about what happened, I'll be waiting up. I love you, best friend, and I will always be here for you," Keesha expressed with tears ready to spill.

"Okay. You got it. But only because you're showing a side of you that I don't get to see." I gave Keesha a hug and went inside of the bathroom. I loved Keesha to the moon and back for this gesture. She was the kind of best friend that most females wished to have. Or they do, and then they end up fucking it over listening to he say/she say bullshit.

I climbed out of my clothes and had one foot in the tub when Keesha came through the door carrying a bath towel. Her face dropped and her mouth hung open as her eyes ogled me from head to toe. She finally said, "Korrin, did you see your fucking body?"

I looked down at my lower half. Red welts were on my legs and were slowly turning purple. There was a full-length mirror in my bathroom and I made my way to look at myself. There were welts everywhere. I used my index finger to touch one and winced because it was painful. Immediately, I cried. What kind of monster would do this? Naked and all, Keesha wrapped her arms around me and the only thing I could do was cry. In the distance I heard my phone ringing, and I just knew it was Sheek.

"Tell me what happened? When I spoke to you about you staying, you were fine," Keesha asked, helping me get inside of the tub.

While the warm water soothed my aches, I went through the whole night, even the part with Shan and Sean, and cried as I visualized Sheek attacking me again.

"I should have listened to Sean right then and there and left right along with them. This is my fault. I should've listened."

Keesha grabbed my chin in her hand and made me look at her. She said, "You better not let those words slip out of your mouth ever again! It is never the woman's fault in a situation like this. You did nothing wrong! You are a beautiful, smart, and strong woman who just fell for a sick man! You hear me! This is not your fault! Don't you ever say that shit again!"

Watching the tears from Keesha's eyes fall started a chain reaction and I began crying again. Keesha left the towel hanging in the bathroom and left me in there. I needed to process what the hell happened. Sheek was a very nice, sweet, kindhearted person, but abuse was a nono on the top of my list.

Standing up in the tub, I drained the water and put the shower on to wash up. When I got out, Keesha had placed my night clothes on my bed and was facing the wall sleeping.

Thank you, God, for giving me Keesha as a best friend, I thought.

Mimi

Chapter Twelve

June 2016

Ever felt so sorry?
All you did was worry
You didn't want nobody,
Thought it would get better

"Go Mom! Go Mom!" Iyana yelled as I walked into the living room.

I had made it to graduation day and my nerves were on fire. My whole family showed up, even Tahjae.

After that night that Sheek put his hands on me, he called my phone nonstop until he gave up and just came over to my house. Keesha answered the door and told him that I wasn't home. She said that he seemed confused about why he had woken up to his window open with my belongings still there. When he was gone, he sent me texts asking to let him know what he did wrong and why I wasn't answering. A few days passed when I decided to text him back letting him know that I needed time and that I would call him.

Here it was six months later and I still hadn't called or texted him. It was tempting because I was so used to texting him throughout my day. It didn't help that he texted me every day. Telling me that he loved me and that he was sorry for what he had done. Even though he didn't exactly know what it was he had done. He still told me I was beautiful. Every day, for six months, even if I didn't respond.

"Are you ready?" Keesha asked.

"I guess."

"Ain't no guessing, bitch. This is what you've been waiting for. Go walk across that stage and make everyone proud."

Keesha said. Her belly was poking out and looked like she was ready to pop. My goddaughter was due in August and I was more than ready to meet her.

Climbing into the BMW X5 that Keesha had rented for the day, we made our way to Proctors. My family was already there seated and waiting on us. In just a few short hours, I would be the first college graduate in my family. And while I was proud that I was graduating, I was most proud of being the first to do so.

***

"Congratulations to the graduating class of 2016!" the dean yelled as every graduate whooped and hollered and celebrated in making it.

I congratulated my fellow classmates and took my gown off to head to the parking lot to meet up with my family. I was killing it in a blush pink spaghetti strap asymmetric dress with nude pumps. My hair was up in a bun with wand curls as my bang. Diamond stud earrings adorned my ears and a diamond chandelier necklace laid on my neck and stopped in between my breasts. Nobody couldn't tell me that I wasn't killing it. My dress clung to every curve that I had due to a semidrastic weight drop. When I got to the parking lot, I spotted them with ease due to the plethora of balloons and the loud music that blasted from their cars.

"Yessss! You killed that stage!" Tahjae yelled and gave me a hug. This was the nature of our relationship. We wouldn't speak after a hug blow up, no one apologizes, and it takes an event to occur for either one of us to start talking to one another.

"So, what's the move now?" I asked.

"Mommy said that she was going to put food on the grill. She invited people from Brooklyn and they should be arriving soon. Tahjae and I gonna go get them and Mommy gonna start the food," Thomasina stated.

"Okay. Sounds like a plan."

The noise from the graduation drowned out the fact that someone was approaching me from behind. I only realized it when everyone got quiet and their attention was drawn to what or rather, who was standing behind me. I turned to a complete surprise.

"Oh my God! Shan, what are you doing here?" I asked. She stood there dressed in jeans, a Vneck polo, and sneakers. She was holding a bouquet of pink perfection, pink roses, pink Asiatic lilies, white alstroemeria, and a white and black gift bag that said "Congrats Grad!"

"First, congratulations on graduating. I'm proud of you, even if we've only met once. Second, the gift and flowers are from Sheek. He's been a mess without speaking to you. I tried to talk him out of coming today, but he was pretty adamant about watching you go across the stage. He knew how important this moment was for you and he knew that he had to witness it, even if it was from yards away. Accept these gifts from him. Those were his words, and not mine. Sheek isn't perfect. Just allow him to explain somethings to you, in order for you to understand. His intentions are never to hurt you. Just listen to him, please," Shan pleaded.

I didn't have the time for this, but I also haven't told my family that Sheek and I had separated on bad terms. That I just needed to focus on my school work. Against my better judgement, I agreed.

"Y'all can go ahead to the house. I'll grab an Uber. Let me speak with Sheek for a second," I said, turning towards my family.

"Korrin… I don't think that's a good idea," Keesha stated. Shan grilled Keesha and Keesha returned the favor.

"I'll be fine, Kee. I'll meet y'all back at the house," I said.

I gave her a look that seemed to settle her just a little. I gave her my cap and gown as she turned around and walked away with everyone else. Shan started to walk away and I followed her.

Sheek was parked not too far from where we were parked. Sean was standing outside of the car on his phone, but hung up when he saw us approaching.

"Congrats, Korrin," he said and grabbed me into a hug.

"Thank you," I responded.

"Big baby waiting on you in the car."

I chuckled and said, "Oh stop."

"No, for real. I've barely seen that man cry in his adult life but for the last six months, he cried almost every day like a bigass baby. Snot bubbles and all."

I couldn't help but laugh harder. I made eye contact with Sheek through the windshield and there was a sadness in his eyes that I've never seen in any grown man. Exhaling, I held onto my flowers and gift and proceeded to the passenger side of the car. When I closed the door, his eyes were lit up like a kid on Christmas morning.

"Congratulations," he said. His voice was doing something to me and melting my heart. Just that one word made me miss hearing his voice, missing him.

"Thank you. You didn't have to come."

"I know I didn't. But I know how hard you worked to get here. And even if we weren't talking, I had to still show support whether you knew or not."

"I appreciate it."

The car got quiet. I didn't say anything because I wasn't the cause of why we were here now. I wasn't the one who wanted to talk; he was. Besides, Shan said to listen, not talk. My mouth was staying shut until he started talking and I was done listening.

"Look at me, Korrin," Sheek said.

I took a few seconds to get my breathing under control. Finally, I looked at him and he continued.

"Korrin, for the longest, I didn't understand why you left my house through the window, in the cold, and why I woke up in a chair blocking the door. Not until a few days later, when I received pictures through texts from an unknown number, of your bruises and a message telling me to stay away from you or the police would be called. Which explains why I just texted you all the time. I took my chances coming here today, but I needed to be here. I am sorry for what I have done. I don't remember doing it. Sad to say that this has happened before."

"What do you mean it's happened before?" I asked. If this man was apologizing and proving that he wanted to change, telling me that it happened before wasn't the way to do it.

"Well, the first time it happened was with my ex from years ago. The first time, she left me and I didn't know why. Weeks went past and I ran into her and as I was asking her how she was doing, she tried to rush away. She didn't want to make any eye contact with me. And when I asked her why, she told me that she was afraid that I would put my hands on her again. I was shocked that she said that. I thought that she was bullshitting, so I let her be.

"I was alone for a long time until I met my first love. We were together up until my father killed my mother. Every other day, I had noticed that she would have a new bruise on her body and the brightness that she held in her eyes was dimming. One day, I had woken up on the couch and it was odd to me because I knew when I went to bed, it was in the bedroom. I got up from the couch and went to the bedroom and was faced with what I had done. She was sitting on the bed crying, hair all over her head, swollen bruised eyes, scratches all over the place, her nails ripped off, and her legs were covered in bruises. When she realized that I was standing there, she looked at me and said that I needed to seek help.

"I broke down and cried. I dropped to my knees and apologized profusely. Any other woman would have run from me. She told me in great detail about what happened and what she described was a complete monster. She told me that I called her Mildred and that I was accusing her of cheating on me with my friends. I couldn't believe it. She told me that I wasn't myself. That I had a crazed look in my eyes. She said that she would forgive me and stay as long as I got help. She said that she was going to be by my side. And she was.

"She was with me when I went to go see a doctor, she was with me through my therapy sessions, and she was with me through my diagnosis."

When Sheek was done, he had tears in his eyes. While he was speaking I heard heartbreak, hurt, regret, and even some fear in his voice. I felt for him. My own tears fell from my eyes. It's not every day that you get a man to open up in this way. To show his emotions. All I wanted to do was grab him into a hug so tight that he would have to push me off of him. Instead I took in everything that he said.

"You said that she stayed with you through your diagnosis. What were you diagnosed with?" I asked. I needed to know.

"Dissociative identity disorder. Also known as"

"Multiple personality disorder," I finished for him. Sheek turned his attention to me and took my hand into his. I allowed it.

108

"Korrin, I apologize from the deepest part of my heart. I should have been honest from the very beginning so that you could have made the choice to still deal with me. There is so much that I would have changed just to stop that from happening. I love you so much. I don't want to lose you, but there is nothing that I could do to control that part of me."

"What about your meds?"

"I take them as prescribed. They help, but sometimes...not."

"So? How many personalities do you have?" I asked. Sheek moved in his seat uncomfortably, but he knew he had to be honest fully with me.

"It's one other, but the one that you saw was the dominant one. He is basically my father. The things I saw him do to my mother were horrible. My therapist told me that I developed his personality when I was young. Said that it was because my father was controlling and showed power that I, Shameek, didn't possess."

"You called me Mildred. Who is Mildred?"

"Mildred was my mother."

The car was quiet. This was a lot to process and I didn't know how to feel about it. Everything in my body told me to leave this nigga alone but my heart...my heart told me to be there for him. To give him an ear when he needed it or a shoulder. That was the best that I could do.

"What happened to your ex?"

"She committed suicide. She left a note saying she forgave me, but she didn't want to live no longer because she was in constant depression. That there was nothing that a doctor could help her with." He cried harder. I placed my flowers on the dashboard and my gift bag between my feet. Reaching over to him, I grabbed him into a hug and tightly squeezed him. This man had years of hurt bottled in him. How could I just abandon him when he is so broken? I asked myself.

"We will get through this," I whispered in his ear. Knowing I should have listened to my gut, I stupidly followed my heart.

For ten minutes, we sat in silence, thoughts running through both of our heads. Eventually he started the car and drove me to my house. As bad as I wanted to invite him in, I told him that it would be best if I got up with him later on. I had to break the news to Keesha. She was hormonal and I needed to prepare myself. This was going to be fun.

Chapter Thirteen

Oh, hey yeah baby
I fear sometimes in my mind
That you won't want to stay with my love
Oh baby

After the barbeque get together, while I should have been sleeping off my drunkenness, my mind was on Sheek. I texted him periodically but as I got undressed to climb into bed, I saw his spare key sitting on my nightstand. Making a rash decision, I got dressed again and woke my mom up to let her know that I would be back in the morning. I called for an Uber and made my way to his house.

It was only eleven when I reached his house. As I exited the Uber, I looked up at his apartment and his bedroom light was on. I made my way inside of the building and walked up the two flights to get to his apartment. My heart beat out of my chest as I inserted the key and unlocked the door.

Click! Clack!

"Who the fuck is that?" Sheek said from the bedroom. The sound of him cocking his gun made my blood run cold and my body shiver.

"It's me." I said quickly. No need for him to step out of the room spraying bullets and asking questions later.

Sheek came out of the room in just his boxers and socks. He stood at the doorway and I dropped the key and ran into his arms. He caught me as I bounced on the balls of my feet and leapt into his arms, wrapping my legs around his waist. His arms rested under my ass, hands on the back of his head, and our tongues dancing with each other.

"I know that you said that we were going to work through it, but I didn't think it was going to be this soon," Sheek expressed as he walked towards the couch and sat down.

"It's already been too long, I can't wait any longer. I missed you," I replied. I placed my lips on his while holding onto the sides of his face.

"I missed you too. Only God knows how much I've missed you."

Sheek lifted me up a tad to get comfortable. His dick had gotten hard and just the thought of him pumping in and out of me made my pussy wet. Sheek helped me take my shirt off and he inhaled my scent by smothering his face between my breasts. I managed to move away from him and stand up.

Sheek looked up at me in confusion. I turned my back and pulled my pants down, wiggling my ass in his face. A smirk appeared on his face as he rubbed his dick through his boxers. Next my shirt and bra came off. Fully naked, I ran my hands over my body and stared intentionally at Sheek. I wanted him in the worst way. My hands cupped my breasts and then slid them down my body and between my legs, my hand coming out dripping wet. I placed my fingers in my mouth, tasting myself. Sheek pulled his boxers off and walked to me, his dick at full attention. When he was close enough to me, he wrapped his arms around me and filled his hands with my ass.

His lips were on mine in a matter of seconds as his hands traveled across my body. Our bodies sank to the floor, mine under his, his fingers working their way inside of my folds. My hips gyrated on his fingers as if it was his dick in me. My hands went to my titties and couldn't help but to rub and squeeze them. My nipples were rock hard and my pussy was overflowing with my juices.

"Damn, babe, you mad wet," Sheek whispered in my ear.

"I told you I missed you," I replied. His fingers slid across my clit, making my back arch and eyes roll to the back of my head.

"This is what you missed?" Sheek asked as he tapped the head of his dick against my pussy lips.

"Yessss," I moaned.

"Tell me you miss this dick," Sheek demanded.

Opening my eyes, I looked at Sheek and said, "I miss that dick."

Sheek got on his knees and grabbed me by my thighs to pull me closer to him. Holding his dick, he entered me, whispering "fuck" as he got comfortable. I felt his dick throbbing. He licked me from my stomach to my breasts, sucking on each nipple, and up to my neck. His hand wrapped around my neck, applying the right amount of pressure to send me into a different state of euphoria. His lips came down on mine as he moved inside of me with smooth, even strokes, pleasure tingling all over my body.

Sheek got up back on his knees and with his dick still in me, he situated himself on the balls of his feet, lifting my legs onto his shoulders.

"Oh God! Yes babe!" I moaned.

"You love me?" he asked, speaking through clenched teeth.

"Yes! You know I love you, Shameek!"

"You gonna leave me again?"

"No, baby! I'm not going anywhere."

"Promise me."

"I promise I'm not going anywhere!" I moaned out loud. My conscience was telling me that I shouldn't have made that type of promise but at that current moment, the dick he was delivering was too fucking good to not say it.

"Turn over," he growled.

I did what he asked and made sure that my ass was high in the air. He got behind me, placing his dick inside of me, being a little rougher this time. My pussy farted as he held me by my waist and slammed into me. My moans were bouncing off of the walls and I could only imagine that his neighbors were getting off by hearing the pleasure that he was giving me.

Sheek's pace increased as he stroked his fingers through my hair and tugged. Shit, this is the best dick he has ever given me, I thought. I heard him whispering "damn" and "fuck" under his breath as his dick pushed back my organs.

"Ooh, I'm cumming, Sheek," I moaned.

"You gonna come all over this dick?"

"Yes," I answered.

And as I did so, he took his dick out of me leaving my pussy, pulsating, ready to cum. I turned over onto my back and looked at him angrily. He walked to the kitchen with a smirk on his face as he grabbed a bottle of water from the fridge and guzzled. My mouth hung open as I watched him come back into the living room and sit on the couch.

"Come sit on my lap," he requested as he pointed to his dick, which was glistening with my juices.

I got up from the floor and sauntered over to Sheek. He leaned against the back of the couch and spread his legs to that I could sit on top of him comfortably. I placed my legs and squatted over him, my pussy hovering over his dick. Looking at him, I lowered myself into him and took every inch of inside of me. My eyes rolled to the back of my head as the feeling coursing through me was unexplainable. His thrusts met my bounce perfectly as his hands grabbed both of my ass cheeks.

"This is all yours, you know, that right?" he questioned.

"Yes, I know," I moaned, my body shaking at the anticipation of cumming all over his dick.

"Are you gonna cum all over this dick again?"

"Ooh yes. I'm 'bout to cum again now."

"Wait for daddy, 'cause I'm ready to cum too."

With a quickness, Sheek lifted me up and pushed me over the couch and pounded himself inside of me deeply. He pushed my head into the cushion as his foot rested in the cushion next to my waist. My pussy had to have been at its wettest as his dick slid in and out of me.

"You better not ever leave me again. Do you understand?" he growled.

I felt his dick throbbing inside of me yet again as I knew he was ready to bust. I moaned my response and his strokes became shorter as he grunted and he released his seeds inside of me. Sheek crumpled to the floor as I curled up onto the couch and tried to stop the dots from floating in front of my eyes.

Just when I thought Sheek was done, he got up from the floor and extended his hand out to me. His dick was up again. He invited me into the shower and stupidly, I went. My pussy ached, but it had been months since I felt him inside of me and it was time to make up for the loss. And besides, Mama didn't raise no punk!

Mimi

Chapter Fourteen

July 2016

What's the point of a relationship
If every other day we gotta save that shit?
It's gotta be love, thought we found it
Ship has been sinking we both have been drowning

It happened again. And this time it was worse. I didn't think that it would, but when it did, I knew that we had to get help sooner rather than later. More so for him, and I was stupidly willingly going to go with him. He was spaced out again when he threw me to the floor and kicked me in my stomach. For weeks, I had to cover up bruises from my kids and Keesha. I made it my business to go and seek counseling because just the medicine wasn't working.

Keesha's due date was coming soon and I had been preparing for her baby shower when she decided to barge in and make herself at home. I had everything scattered around the coffee table.

"Can this baby come the fuck out already? It's too fucking hot to be lugging around this damn belly everywhere," Keesha exclaimed while falling onto the couch

"Girl, you got a few more weeks until that baby ready to come out. You can wait it out."

Keesha huffed and then asked, "Where the kids?"

"I sent them to Thomasina. I needed a damn break."

"What they do now?"

"Nothing. Life is just moving too fast."

Keesha's face got serious as she asked, "How are things between you and Sheek?"

Exhaling, I looked up at her and answered honestly. I said, "I think we need to see a therapist."

"What for?"

For these bruises that I have across my back. For the bruises that I am sure will come in the near future because I'm too stupid to leave him, I thought to myself. Instead of saying exactly what was in my mind, I said, "Because I think there are things that we both need to work on if we want to be together in the long run."

"Is he putting his hands on you again?"

"Keesha, no. Because I want to seek therapy doesn't mean that that is the case. Sheek had stated that he wanted to get married in the future and if I see myself being with him, then I want to make sure that we are both mentally prepared for it."

"Are you serious?"

"What?"

"After he put his hands on you that one time, you're considering marrying him? I thought you were crazy for taking him back but you are straight up delusional to marry him."

"Kee, it's nothing that is set in stone. I'm not running off to go marry him today or tomorrow."

Keesha sat up in her seat, her belly round like a basketball between her legs. She asked, "What if therapy doesn't work? Huh? What are you going to do then? Are you thinking about the type of exposure you are going to put the kids through? Korrin, you are not one of these dumb broads, but it seems like you done lost your way a little bit and a screw or two."

"Kee, you don't understand."

She rose to her feet, hands on her hips, and yelled, "So help me understand, Korrin! Am I supposed to sit here and watch you kill yourself by being with this nigga? Who's gonna be there for the kids? Their fathers ain't shit! Who's gonna be here to help me raise my baby?"

The tears fell from Keesha's eyes and I finally realized what the real issue was. She wasn't worried about nothing but who was going to help her raise her baby. She never disclosed to me who the baby's father was, so I made a vow to step in just like she did with my kids. Some people would call it selfish but, in all reality, she was scared. And I got it. I knew how she felt times a thousand.

"Whoa, whoa, whoa! Kee, I know you scared, babes, but I will make sure that you are not alone in this. I will be there for you every step of the way. There is no need for you to be stressing this way. The baby is going to be here sooner than you think and I don't need you getting emotional with me now. Look, sit back down and help me with these ribbons."

I grabbed Keesha into my arms for a hug. She dried her eyes and sat down on the couch again. The baby shower was in a couple of days and I needed all of the help that I could get. And Kee needed to get her mind occupied because I didn't need her melting down like that again.

***

Later on, that night, Sheek came over to have dinner with myself and the kids. They loved when he came around because my rules basically didn't apply as he played the game system with them, fed them sweets, and rolled around the damn house like he was a kid too. I allowed it because it was only two days out of the week that he comes over to have dinner with us.

"Okay, kids! Time to do chores," Sheek mentioned. It was almost bed time and chores and showers needed to done.

With ease, the kids got up and began doing what needed to be done. Sheek came back inside of the living room and sat next to me on the couch.

"You okay?" he asked.

"Yes. Why do you ask?"

"You look like you got something on your mind."

A small smile came across my lips because he knew me so well. I said, "Well, I do. I was hoping to speak with you about it later but the kids are busy and out of earshot. So, I don't see why not now."

"Okay. Go for it."

"You know how you told me that your ex had sat with you through your therapy sessions? Well, I was talking with a coworker and she had mentioned that there is a therapist that she knows that does free sessions on Saturdays and I was wondering if you would be willing to go?"

Sheek was silent and I didn't know how he felt about the situation. His face was unreadable and my heart pounded in my chest because I didn't know what he was thinking.

"You were talking about me to your coworkers?" he asked.

"No. We were talking in general about how we could help families that need therapy but can't afford it. Then she remembered that she knew a therapist who did free sessions. I think that we should try it out."

Sheek straightened himself up on the couch and cleared his throat. He looked at me and said, "Are you sure?"

"Yes, I am. There are some things that I'd like to discuss with you that may be hard for me to discuss and I think that a therapist would help. Not only me, but you as well. I just want us to both be open about this if our relationship is worth fighting for to make it better."

"Okay. I know Keesha's baby shower is this Saturday, so make an appointment for next Saturday."

"Really? Are you serious?" I didn't think that it would be this easy for me to get him to agree. Whether it was this easy or any harder, as long as he said yes and was open to the idea, I was okay with it.

"Yes. I know how much this would mean to you and I know that when I was with my ex, it helped me a lot. I had less blackout episodes and I had a grip on my life. So, let's do it."

Going in asking him, I was a nervous wreck. Knowing that he was with the idea was like a weight was lifted off of my shoulders. I jumped into his arms, hugged him tight, and thanked him for being open about it. He chuckled and placed kisses on my face.

"You better stop before you start something. The kids are up and the way you hugging on me would be cause for me to dig you out," Sheek whispered in my ear.

I pushed myself off of him and said, "Ugh, you can be so corny sometimes."

Julian stuck his head out of the kitchen and said, "Mom can we pop some popcorn and watch a movie?"

"Yes, but it's bed right after," I responded.

A chorus of yes's came from the kitchen as a smile spread on Sheek's face. They were lucky I needed to finish the party favors for the baby shower.

***

Saturday came faster than what I expected and I was still running around like a chicken with my head chopped off. Thomasina and Tahjae came over to help me with the decorations and cook. I had to run out and get the cake and an outfit. The baby shower started at one and Keesha was supposed to arrive at onethirty. Knowing Keesha, she would already be there touching shit and getting in the way.

On my way back to my house, Sheek called me to see how things were going.

"Like there aren't enough hours in the day to get the little bit of shit I gotta do, to get done," Was my response.

"Relax, babe. You got everything under control. You stressing and worrying over minor shit. What else do you need to get done?"

"I just went to go get the cake and now I'm heading to Marshall's to grab some shoes and an outfit. My sisters are at the house decorating and cooking."

"You need me to do anything?"

"Yeah, show up. That's it."

"You think that's a good idea? You know Keesha don't fuck with me."

"Keesha knows that we are working on repairing our relationship. Bring a gift and she will be okay."

The phone got silent and just as I was about to check if he was still there, he began speaking. He said, "No one has believed in me as much as you do. Not even my ex. At least, I don't believe that she did. Even in my dark times, you believe in me, and I just wish that there was a cure for this shit. I don't want to be this way."

"Your ex did all that she could to help you and I know she believed in you. She just lost her way in believing in herself while helping you. All she wanted was to make sure that you were well, but lost herself in the process. I could only imagine what you go through during that moment. There's no cure but we can do therapy and meds to hold it at bay and that's the next best thing. Like I said, we gonna get through this no matter what."

"Thank you, babe. I'm gonna let you go so you could concentrate on doing your thing. I'll see you at the baby shower."

"Okay. I love you."

"I love you too."

When we hung up, I walked into Marshall's and went to the dresses. They were picked over and barely anything stood out. I went through a bunch of dresses before I found the one. It was buried deep like someone was hiding it for themselves, but I ended up finding it. It was a red off the shoulder dress with sleeves and stopped midthigh. The sleeves didn't bother me because we were gonna be in the A.C. and the dress was simple enough to not upstage the mommytobe. Next up was the shoe department. Instantly, I saw a pair of open toe heels with a clear strap over the toes and a strap around the ankles. Fifteen minutes later, and I was making my way through my door.

My living room was covered in pink. Pink streamers, pink balloons, pink wall decorations with baby Minnie Mouse on them. I had rented white chairs for the guests and there were pink decorations on those too. I bought Keesha a white throne chair instead of renting it so that she could put it inside the baby's room. That was placed in the corner with pink and white balloons with "Congrats" and "It's a girl" written on them. The party favors and ribbons were placed on a table along the wall with a space for the cake.

Thomasina and Tahjae were in the kitchen throwing down when I slid through the kitchen to put my things down in my room.

"You got everything?" Tahjae asked with a cup in her hand. I just knew that it was alcohol.

"Yeah. I just got to go back out to the car and get the cake."

"I got it. You start getting ready. The kids are all done and Keesha tried to bring her happy ass in here, but I stopped her and told her to go finish getting her hair done."

I rolled my eyes because I knew she was going to do that. I said, "Thank you. Is the food almost done?"

"Yeah. Thomasina is making the last little bit of fried chicken."

"Okay, cool. I'm gonna jump in the shower." I looked at the time and it was already twelve. Rushing to the bathroom with my towel, I stole a piece of chicken to feed my grumbling stomach. By the time I was done in the bathroom, it was closer to one and I was rushing. One of my sisters turned the music on and opened the front door, leaving the screen door closed.

Thank God I decided to get my hair done a few days prior. When I was dressed, I combed my hair down and flat ironed the ends. I was rocking a twentyinch jet black weave. I placed my diamond studs in my ears and spritzed on some Viva La Juicy Gold Couture on my body and went to help out with what was left.

Keesha promptly showed up at onethirty like I knew she would. She looked beautiful in a pink baby doll dress, comfy white Steve Madden slides that had pink fur on the strap across the top of her foot, and her hair was slayed to the Gawds in medium beach curls.

"Aww, you look so beautiful," I said as I gave her a hug.

"I feel miserable," she responded with a straight face.

"Stop it. At least you can sit the whole time and look pretty while we cater to you."

"I'd rather be sleeping."

"Keesha, go sit your ass down with your extra ass."

Huffing and puffing, Keesha went to go have a seat in her chair.

As hostess, I let everybody mingle for the first half hour and then got the games under way. We played "Guess that candy" where we rubbed different kinds of chocolate candy inside of diapers and the playing participants had to lick it to identify what kind it was. The winner would receive a prize. Sheek showed up with Charles halfway through "Winner takes all", a game where playing participants put whatever amount of money inside of a bowl and had to guess or come close to the mommytobe number and they would win not the money in the bowl, but the laundry detergent All. It was my favorite baby shower game 'cause the winner thinks they are taking the bowl of money when in all actuality that money goes to the parent for baby.

We began to serve the food so that Keesha could open her gifts. She was beginning to look uncomfortable by the look on her face and I just wanted to make sure that she got some rest. I went into the kitchen to make me a drink. Thomasina and Tahjae were there and conversation ceased when I arrived.

"What's going on in here?" I asked. The saying goes that if the conversation stops when you enter, the conversation was most likely about you. The guilty look on Tahjae's face confirmed it.

"Nothing. Your sister here was just telling me that Charles is Keesha's baby father," Thomasina said, rolling her eyes. That look told me how silly she thought the information was.

"Girl, what? When you get some drink in your system, you always talking out the side of your neck. Why do you think Charles is her baby father?" I asked with my hand on my hip.

"No one, not even you, her best friend, knows who her baby father is. So it makes perfect sense for her not to tell you. He is the only guy here besides your nigga, and look how he over there whispering in her ear."

I turned my attention to Charles and Keesha. He was talking in her ear, but that was because the music was loud. I was barely able to hear these two, so that didn't mean anything.

"Girl, bye, I could barely hear you with the music on. They in the room with the music playing, so I could only imagine them not hearing each other," I answered while finishing up my drink.

"Why are you always taking up for her?"

"How am I taking up for her, Tahjae? You're clearly trying to make something out of nothing."

"And that is exactly how you're taking up for her. You treat her like she's your sister more than your blood sisters."

Thomasina, usually the levelheaded one, stepped in between us. She said, "Right now isn't the right time for this."

"No, she feels a certain way, let's get this shit out in the open. Speak on it, sis," I said. I was just about through with Tahjae and her antics.

"Korrin, it's really not the right time and I really wish that you could be the bigger person and drop it."

Tahjae stood on the other side of the kitchen with a smirk on her face and I just knew I needed to leave it alone. That smirk only meant that she was doing shit on purpose. Today was about my best friend and I didn't want to ruin her day.

"Babe! Korrin!" I heard Sheek calling my name. He came inside of the kitchen and grabbed my arm to drag me into the kitchen. The guests of the baby shower were crowded around Keesha and Charles had a look of fear on his face. I turned the music off and made my way to Keesha's side.

"Kee? You okay?" I asked.

"No, bitch! I'm having a contraction. I've been having them all day, but this one is the worst," she answered.

"Why didn't you tell me? I would have cancelled the baby shower."

"What kind of friend would I be if I made you do that after everything that you have done?" she panted. I needed to get her to the hospital.

"Sheek, I need you to drive us to the hospital. Thomasina, can you do something with this party? And Charles, can you bring all of her gifts to her apartment? Her key is the blue one that's on my key ring," I ordered while trying to get Keesha to stand up and walk.

"Fuck you mean I bring her stuff? I'm going to the hospital too," Charles said.

Tahjae yelled from the kitchen, "I told your dumb ass so!"

I looked between Keesha and Charles. I couldn't believe this shit. Shaking my head, I continued to help Keesha to the car. Charles picked her up and placed her in the back seat of Sheek's car. Sheek and I climbed in and within seconds, we were speeding down the block, heading towards the hospital. The car was quiet and as much as I wanted to make sure that Keesha was okay, I was furious. How could they do this behind my back? Keesha knew how I felt about her sleeping with one of my brothers. It was my number one rule. She was an only child so she never had to worry about me sleeping with her brothers.

"Don't be mad at me, Korrin. It only happened once and never was supposed to happen," Keesha said from the back seat.

"That's not what you need to be focused on right now, Kee. Try concentrating on your breathing," I said. Although furious, I still needed to give her my support. I reached my hand to the back seat and held her hand. They were grown and there was nothing that I could do.

Twelve hours later, Dalila Korrin Richards was born at exactly 4:27 in the morning. She was healthy, weighing seven pounds ten ounces. She was born with a full head of hair and looked exactly like my brother. One look at her and my heart melted, forgetting all about what Keesha and Charles had done to create her. Keesha was out of it after giving birth, but she apologized continuously. Of course I'd forgiven her.

Dalila was more than my godchild. She was my niece, and for that I thanked Keesha and told her that Dalila was the greatest gift that she could give me. Who was I to be mad when there was a child involved?

Crime of Passion 3

Chapter Fifteen

I don't wanna be this woman
The second time around
'Cause I'm waking up screaming, no longer believing
That I'm gonna be around

School for the kids was back in session and I had begun working full time. My weekends were free for me to do whatever it is that I wanted to do and oftentimes it was me going over to Sheek's house to make sure that we attended therapy together. We'd had three sessions since Keesha gave birth to my niece and it seemed like it was working. Sheek hadn't had a blackout since before the baby shower.

Tahjae had taken the kids for the weekend and I spent my time with Sheek at his house. The day of going to see our therapist, I woke up in a good mood. Sheek had laid the pipe down the night before and that earned him the breakfast that I was making before we went to go see Ms. Daniels.

"It smells good in here," Sheek said, walking up behind me, wrapping his arms around my waist and placing a kiss on my cheek.

"Thank you. It's almost done."

"Good, 'cause a nigga is hungry."

I giggled and Sheek went to take a seat in front of the TV. Five minutes later, I was fixing our plates. Realizing that time was moving fast, we rushed to eat, shower, and dress. This session was important to me. I was fully opening up to Sheek about how I truly felt, things about my past, and shit that I struggle with on an everyday basis. This would be my first time letting my guard down to anyone I've dated. This was a twoway street and if I expected him to be open, I needed to be open as well.

"Hello, Ms. Richards and Mr. Scott. How are you today?" Ms. Daniels asked as she invited us into her office.

"We're doing good," Sheek answered.

"Okay. Let's jump right into it then. Ms. Richards, after the last session, you asked me if you could have the floor. That you wanted to speak with Mr. Scott about things that you have went through, things that you have to battle with within yourself every day. You will be able to do so, and I will be here taking notes, and if you struggle with anything, I'm here to help."

I smiled and thanked her. I turned on the couch so that I was facing Sheek. I wanted us to have the most eye contact so that I could read him, and he could exchange the same thing. The love that he held in his gaze made my heart pound in my chest. I searched my thoughts to figure out where I should begin.

"I walk around like I don't have a single care in the world and this air of confidence that I truly don't have. Every day I'm constantly beating myself up on the inside about every single detail of my life. If I discipline the kids, I second guess myself on if I was being too harsh or if it was the right thing to do. Or if I had an idea about something that pertains to becoming a better person, I overthink too much, which causes me to stress. I try to change this because I know I don't need to be too hard on myself, but it's something that I have a hard time shaking. I lack confidence and for years, I was able to make it seem like I believed it. I selfcriticize myself all the time. I question why I would wear something knowing there is a roll or two hanging out. And I hate it."

"Oh, babe, you are the most beautiful woman walking this earth," Sheek interrupted.

I blushed and continued, "And when you say things like that, I should be feeling like I am, but I'm really feeling thinking, am I really? That's something that I need to work on with myself. No matter how many times you tell me that I am beautiful, I'm always going to second guess, and that is nothing on you.

"Growing up, hearing fat ass this and fat ass that destroyed my confidence before I even made it into adulthood, and no one cared. Sad to say that that's how it is in black households. We are taught to show tough love. It destroyed me internally.

"A few years ago, I was diagnosed with depression. I didn't even know I had it. Julian's father called CPS on me and when they entered my apartment, it was all bad. The house was so filthy that they had no choice but to remove the kids, arrest me, and close down my apartment. The fact that Julian's father called CPS on me had nothing to do with my living conditions. He was upset that he was caught smoking PCP again and I refused to let him see the kids. I guess him calling CPS on me was a blessing because it woke me up. I needed to get my shit together. I saw a therapist then and I had been diagnosed with it for years."

My chest was starting to feel heavy as the air in the room felt like it was getting thick. I felt my face becoming red with embarrassment. I mean, who wants to admit that their living conditions were so bad that their kids had to be removed, got arrested, and code shut down the apartment. Looking up at Sheek, he still had the loving look in his eyes. He grabbed ahold of my hand and squeezed it tight, letting me know that it was okay to continue.

"When I was young, I think maybe around four was when it all began. My mother was dating this guy and from that early age, I knew that he was off. It started off with him making me sit on his lap. It slowly graduated to him secretly grabbing my hand and placing it on his crotch area. When he would be giving everyone a hug to leave, he'd pinched my nipple and kiss my mouth, sticking his tongue in my mouth in the process.

"I never told anyone because I didn't know no better. I remember he was fixing my clothes one time. I had on pink corduroy pants and I think a lightcolored shirt. He stood me on top of the kitchen counter and began fixing my pants. Before he zipped up my pants, he looked up at me and mouthed shhh, winked his eye, and stuck his tongue in and licked the top of my panties." I had to pause in telling my story because my body was starting to tremble and the tears were cascading down my face. No matter how many times I thought I was over this, telling my story was a reminder that my innocence was taken from me. No, he didn't rape me, but his touching me set off so many things in me at a young age. Ms. Daniels came closer and handed me some tissues. I managed to continue.

"Years continued to fly by and I got bigger and it got worse. He started to take me and my siblings out to the movies, where he made sure that I sat next to him so he could feel on me, or he would take his penis out and make me rub my hand across it. I think that that's when my depression started because I remember being eight years old, talking about wanting to kill myself. I wanted to end my life by jumping in front of a bus. I had suicidal thoughts well into my early twenties."

I cried harder as I mentioned the horrible things that were done to me. I went on to tell Sheek about how he would beat me while I was completely naked and enjoyed it. As a child, I was exposed to this and was always bribed to keep my mouth shut. It was anything from toys, to candy, to money, to jewelry. He always followed through with the things that he said that he was going to give me, so I never thought about opening my mouth. I used to feel like if I would have said something, then it could have ended."

By the time the session ended, my eyes were puffy, my nose had become stuffed up, and my nose was red. Sheek gave me the biggest hug ever and promised me that he would help me through all the things I was going through just like I was helping him. He promised that he would never leave my side ever. For the first time in a long time, I was able to breathe. We thanked Ms. Daniels, and we both walked out of there feeling new. I hope that after today, things would take a turn for the better.

***

"Get the fuck out of the bed!" Sheek yelled while dragging me by the foot.

My eyes flew open and the lower half of my body was already on the floor while my upper half remained on the bed.

"What the fuck?" I questioned in a daze. I was trying to figure out what the hell was going on. Sheek stalked over to me and grabbed a handful of my hair and dragged me into the living room. Just when I thought things were going to be good, they went bad. My hands wrapped around his, trying to get his hands from off my hair.

"I'm gonna fix your ass today!" Sheek yelled. He threw me against the couch, hurting my back in the process.

"Owww. Sheek! It's me, Korrin! Please don't do this!"

Slap!

The sting from the slap burned my skin hot. I was confused for a few seconds, but that didn't stop him from picking me up by my neck and punch me in my gut. Immediately he dropped me, and I struggled to catch my breath. Sheek left from my lime of vision and I took that time to try and pick myself up from the floor. I was bent over pulling myself up when he came back and kicked me in my ass and I fell back down. Okay, Korrin, you need to fight back. This has to stop today, I said to myself.

Sheek grabbed me by my hair again and slammed me on my back. He climbed in top of me and began to choke me. Out of fear and the crazy look that he had in his eyes, I began moving my body to get him off me. He didn't even budge. Seeing that that wasn't working, I began clawing at his face. It took some time, but he finally let me go, but not before he punched me in my mouth and I knew that my lip was busted.

I got up and began to head to the bedroom to get my things to leave. Sheek had a different agenda because I was dragged into the living room yet again.

"No! You're not doing this shit to me again!" I yelled while trying to get his hands off me. We began to tussle and ended up crashing into the TV, causing it to fall from the wall onto the floor. Sheek got ahold of the collar of my shirt and slammed me against the wall, all the while calling me a bunch of bitches and whores.

With all my might, I clenched my fist and delivered a blow so hard to his nose that he was stunned and let me go. I didn't let up either. By far, I wasn't as strong as he was but if this was how it was going to be, then I was fighting until the end. As he held his nose, I delivered a two piece that dropped him to his knees.

"I'm tired of this shit! You want to fight me like I ain't been good to you and try to help you through this! You got me fucked up, Sheek! I swear to God, one of us is leaving in an ambulance, and I promise you that it won't be me!"

Sheek grabbed my legs, sweeping them from under my body. I fell to the floor, banging my elbows on the floor as well as the back of my head. He climbed on top of me and

134

before I knew it, he was slapping me with a skillet. I don't know where the skillet came from, but he made it a point to use it. My face was swelling, and my eye was barely a slit. Sounds like the ocean were ringing in my ear.

"You bitch! I didn't want to do this to you! You just had to go and fuck Doug! Was I not man enough for you!" Sheek yelled.

He was off me now and I was getting up, wielding the same skillet he just hit me with. I swung the skillet with all my might in the back of his head and he went down. Wasting no time, I went into his room, grabbed my shorts from the floor and my shoes. I came flying out of the room, Sheek was standing on the side of the room door. He stuck his arm out, causing me to stop me in my tracks by running my neck into his arm. He picked me up and slammed me against the wall.

I was searching around with my hands for anything that I could get my hands on to hit him with. Nothing was in my reach and he had put his hands around my neck again. I was literally fighting for my life. And then I was able to grab ahold of something. Holding it in my hands, I raised it over my head and slammed the heavy object on his. I watched as his eyes rolled to the back of his head and he slowly dropped to the floor. Dust rained down on both of us. I grabbed my phone from the dresser and left everything else in there.

"Help! Help! Somebody help me!" I yelled while running out of his building. The sun was coming up and somebody had to have been up that would hear me. I ran out into the street, running, pieces of glass getting stuck in the bottom of my feet. It was hard for me to breath and the next thing I remember was the ground reaching up to me.

***

"Just look at her damn face! What do you mean she should have listened to you when he was trying to holla at you? You do remember that that didn't happen, right? Furthermore that has nothing to do with why she is laying in this fucking bed right now!" Keesha spoke in high octaves. I just knew she was talking to Tahjae.

"Whether it happened or not, I knew he wasn't shit from the gate. She should have just been "

"Do you know how insensitive you sound? Nobody could have told her to stop fucking with him. She had to do that on her own and we, as her sister, could have only been there for her."

"Funny you mention sisters when you're really not her sister," Tahjae said with a chuckle.

"Bitch, I've been more than a sister to her than you have. Every chance you get, you argue with her over the dumbest shit."

"You know only what she tells you. And it ain't never the whole truth."

"What she tells me and what you show me adds the fuck up pretty well."

I got tired of them bickering and finally opened my eyes. At least as much as I could with the swelling. I said, "A bitch could be on her death bed and y'all still would argue. Y'all sure y'all not sisters?"

"Oh my God, Korrin! Are you okay?" Keesha asked.

"I guess. I'm alive, right?"

Both Keesha and Tahjae walked closer to me and I could tell from the look on Tahjae's face that I looked jacked up. Who the hell called her ass up here? I thought. I didn't need her type of energy.

"Do you need me to get the nurse?"

"No. I just need some water, and where are the kids?"

"At my house with Charles. Thomasina is on her way. I don't know if your mom is coming up or not."

Tahjae smoothed my hair down and looked at me. Her face had softened, and she weakly smiled. "The police were here, and they wanted to question you, but we told them to come back later when you would be up. Despite Keesha and me bickering, I really am sorry that he did this to you."

"He will get what he deserves. I will make sure of that."

"I'm gonna go get you some water and give Mom a call," Tahjae said, her voice cracking. She rushed out of the room and I looked at Keesha.

"Your sister is so dramatic. If the attention ain't on her, she gonna make sure that it is," Keesha said, shaking her head.

"She been that way all of her life. I don't pay that girl no mind."

Keesha sat on the side pf the hospital bed and rubbed her hand across mine. She couldn't even look at me, and I didn't blame her.

"How did I get here? Last thing I remember I was running down the street screaming for help."

"From what the nurse told me, someone found you unconscious in the street. She called the police and stayed with you until you got here, waited until I got here, and from what I could tell, she's been waiting for you wake up."

"What? Who is she? I don't know anyone around that area."

"Want me to go get her?" Keesha asked.

"I look a mess. I don't think that I could face her looking like this."

"I think that you should, just to thank her. She's been here for hours and I'm sure that she has things to do."

"Okay. And I'm only agreeing because I know that you are gonna keep badgering me about it."

"Good. I'll go get her," Keesha stated as she slid out of the room.

While she was gone, I had just a few minutes alone to get my thoughts together. If only I had left when I had the chance, or if I would have just stayed gone, this wouldn't have happened.

Keesha came back in the room with the woman. She was beautiful, about my height, thick, and had skin the color of burnt caramel. She looked familiar but then again, I was around Sheek's way often and I could have seen her in passing.

"Sorry I look a mess," was the first thing that came from out if my mouth.

"Now there is no need to apologize. I'm just glad that you are okay."

"Thank you for everything. If it wasn't for you, then who knows what would have happened to me?"

"You don't need to thank me. I needed to make sure that you were okay. I'm glad that you are. I know that you need your rest so I'm going to head out. If you need anything, I will leave my card with you. Don't hesitate to call or send a text."

"Oh, wait, I didn't get your name."

"Coincidentally, my name is Angel. Get well soon," she said with a smile on her face.

I returned it and thanked her once again as she turned to leave. Keesha came and sat back on the bed next to me.

"You okay?"

"Yeah. I just want to sleep."

"Go ahead. I'm gonna go get something to eat and see when they will be releasing you."

Nodding my head, I quickly slipped into a slumber and dreamed about the fight that I had with Sheek. Except in my dream, he managed to kill me. When I woke up, there were tears in my eyes and Keesha along with the doctor were looking down at me.

"How long was I asleep for?" I asked.

"Just about an hour, and lucky for you the doctor is here to release you," Keesha stated.

Thank God, I couldn't help but to think. Going home was exactly what I needed. After signing the papers and getting dressed, I was free to go.

***

My house was quiet when I returned. Keesha went down to check on the kids while I headed to take a shower. Thank God for her, she didn't want to lie to the kids, but she told them that I had to go away for a week to buy me some time to heal so they didn't have to see me like this. By the time I was done with my shower, Keesha was in my room with a plate of food. My stomach grumbled, but I didn't have an appetite.

"Did you get that dust off you? Where did it come from anyway?" she asked.

"Chile, that wasn't dust. That was his mama."

Keesha's mouth dropped and she couldn't help but to laugh. I joined in with her and it was the best laugh that I'd had in a long time. At the moment that I was smashing the urn across his head, I didn't realize what it was until I replayed the fight in my head.

"Bitch, you cracked that nigga upside his head with his mama?" Keesha asked, tears of laughter rolling down her cheeks.

"I had to get him off me, Keesha. It was either that or die, and dying wasn't an option for me."

"I'm just glad that you are okay. Do you want to file a police report?"

"Hell yeah."

"Okay get your rest, eat some of this food, and in the morning, we'll go to the police station."

"Okay. Thank you for always coming through."

Keesha hugged me and place a kiss on my forehead. She responded, "That's what family is for. Besides, I'm not pregnant anymore and if he tries to come around then I can kick his ass and shank his ass. Get some rest."

Keesha turned to leave and I continued to get dressed. I was alone with my thoughts. My eyes went to my cell phone that was sitting on my nightstand. Everything in me wanted to check my messages, but I knew if I did that it was going to be bad. So I left it alone. I took Keesha's advice and ate, more so picked at the food that she had brought me. By the time I went to bed, Sheek was on my mind heavy.

Part 3:

After the Storm

Mimi

Chapter Sixteen

January 2018

I'ma keep my head up hold it high
Really did my best God knows you try
Even though it hurts I will survive,
I'll wipe my eyes, I'll say it loud

Leaving Sheek's ass was the best thing I could have done. Upon Keesha's advice, we went the next day to the police station. I cried through the process. They took pictures, made a report, and Keesha provided them with photos that Angel had taken when she found me. A couple of days later they called and told me that they went to his house to arrest him. They said that his door was open, and the house was a mess. He was laying on the couch with a bottle in his hand shedding tears. He willingly went. They showed him the pictures of the damage that he caused. He explained his diagnosis and that he didn't mean to do it. They still locked him up.

My heart broke for him. I know it was stupid of me to care, but I knew that he wasn't himself, but I also felt like what he and I were doing wasn't enough. Keesha advised me to get a lawyer. My lawyer advised that I testify. As much as I didn't want to, I was going to. I've read so many articles about domestic violence that it brought me to tears. So many women were dying at the hands of their abusers and me testifying was a way to bring awareness and to let women know that if ever face with this type of situation, it's okay for you to fight back and leave.

The New Year had come in and the past four months were the hardest I had to endure in my life. Every day I cried. I slipped so deep into depression that Keesha ended up keeping the kids for longer than what it took for me to heal. She called my job and told them what happened, and they were gracious enough to let me take a leave of absence.

Day in and day out, I laid in bed, barely eating, showering, just disconnected from the world. However, I made sure that I spoke to my kids twice a day to assure them that I was okay. What snapped me out of my haze was a visit from Shan and Sean. Thankfully, the day they decided to pop up, I had showered and Keesha had cleaned up. When I opened the door, I was surprised to see them.

"Hey, what are y'all doing here?" I asked and allowed them to come inside.

Shan was the one to speak. She said, "We are here on behalf of Sheek. He sent us to tell you first that he was sorry for what he has done. He said that he would have rather died to have hurt you the way that he did. He asks that you don't testify against him. He says that you know that he wasn't himself."

I was appalled. Whether he wasn't himself or not doesn't excuse what he did. I said, "What? Why wouldn't I testify?"

"Look, I know what he did to you was fucked up. I get that, but I can't have my brother in jail behind this," Shan spoke. She now had her hands on her hips and was giving me attitude.

"Which is why I am testifying. You gonna tell me that if the same thing happened to you, you think your brothers is gonna go tell the nigga you abused to not testify?"

"First of all, I wouldn't be with a nigga that would let me abuse him. That shows me he's weak and I don't fuck with weak men."

"You sound stupid as hell. You need to educate yourself. As a woman you should know that 1 in 4 women and 1 in 9 men experience severe physical violence with their partners.

Instead of saying that you can't have him in jail, you should be encouraging me to have his ass in there. It was either jail or six feet under 'cause as quiet as it's kept, jail wasn't my only option and I didn't have him six feet under 'cause he needs help. He needs to know all there is to having multiple personalities, and he needs to not have negative energy around him egging him on. Did you know that he wishes to not be that way every single day? How often do y'all take the time to talk to him about what he goes through day in and day out? Get out of my house! You got a lot of nerve!"

"Testify and see what's gonna happen," Sean warned.

"Is that a threat? Watch me testify and I swear to God on my kids' lives, both of you will be either six feet under or in jail along with him. I don't know y'all like that, so I could care less which way y'all end up. But I know him, so try me if you want to."

"Coming from a bitch that got her ass and tryna have that nigga in jail," Shan snickered.

Reaching into my robe pocket, I pulled out a pistol and smacked Shan with the butt of the gun, right in the nose. Instantly it was broken, and blood was leaking onto my front porch.

"Y'all will never catch me sleeping after what he did to me. My aim is A1, and I guarantee you that I won't miss. Get the fuck away from my house and if you two come anywhere near me, you better hope they let your brother out for a double funeral," I said, my eyes bouncing between the both of them. My heart was pounding in my chest something crazy and I wanted to cry, but I stood my ground and showed them that I meant business. I didn't know how to use a gun. I had just recently got it for just in case purposes and it came in handy. As I looked at the gun that I held in my hand, they finally decided to turn around and leave.

After their visit, I decided that that was going to be the end of my depression. The things Shan said to me hurt me deep, but it was women like her made me want to get out there and educate.

Keesha came over the next day and saw me up and about and was surprised. I told her everything that happened between myself, Shan, and Sean. Her response was that I should have let her beat Shan's ass at my graduation. I couldn't have allowed that; she was pregnant then. I blamed myself for not knowing that something was up with Shan and Sean. They could have told me what was up when they warned me that there was something up with him.

"Keesha, would it be wrong that I don't want to see him put in jail? That he should be in a mental institution to get the correct help that he needs?" I asked Keesha when she had brought the kids back home. I was curled up on the couch, drinking hot chocolate, under a blanket.

"He needs to be in jail. But that's just my opinion. If you mention that he should be committed to an inpatient program, they may just keep him in there for a year, issue a stay away order for indefinitely, and after the year is up, he will probably have to continue treatment for who knows how long. You know him better than I do, and you have been on the other side of his blackouts, so you know how bad it could be. I think that you should do what is best for you. Whatever it is that will help sleep better at night. Does this have to do with what Shan said about not having him in jail?"

"Absolutely not. I was thinking about this since I last spoke with my lawyer. I think that's why I was beating myself up so much about it."

"Do what's gonna make you feel safe. You and the kids' safety is all that matters."

Keesha was right. The day that I was to testify was coming up faster than what I wanted it to, so I needed to make my decision and speak with my lawyer.

Mimi

Chapter Seventeen

And I'ma be okay
'Cause I'm gonna live my life, my way
And you can say what you wanna say
It won't affect the way I'm living I'm winning by being free
again

The last time I was in a courtroom I vowed to never see the inside of another one for the rest of my life. Being inside of a courtroom made me nervous. I had been in the waiting area for what seemed like an eternity, when the bailiff came into the waiting area and called my name. I walked in and my lawyer was already sitting at the table so I went to join her. Immediately I started picking away at my fingernails out of nervous energy. Keesha was sitting in the pews to show support as well as Thomasina, Tahjae, my mom, and Angel.

"All rise, Judge Allison Brown preceding," the bailiff yelled.

Everyone in the courtroom stood up as the judge came in and took her seat behind the bench. She ordered the bailiff to bring in the defendant, Shameek. The room was silent as the bailiff left through a door and returned with Sheek. He was shackled with full body restraints. The chain wrapped around his waist, went down to his ankles, and up to his wrists. He was dressed in an orange jumpsuit and white skippies.

Almost afraid to look at him in the face, I willed myself to look at him, and what I saw looking back at me broke my heart. Sheek's face was swollen. His eyes were almost shut, scrapes and bruises lined his face. His lips were swollen with caked up blood on the corners. His eyes connected with mine and they were filled with sorrow and an apology. I wondered what the hell happened to his face. The reason why we are here is because of him. Do not feel sorry for him! He deserved what happened to him! the voice in my head screamed. My eyes casted down to the table as I forced myself to not shed a tear.

Court began with my lawyer speaking on my behalf. She described in detail what I told her happened. It was everything from the first time it happened up until the last moment. She presented the pictures to the courtroom that were taken at the police station as well as the ones from Angel that showed me unconscious in the street. Living through the visuals again brought tears to my eyes and everyone in the courtroom, including the judge, who tried to be slick about it.

Sheek, who had decided to defend himself, sat with tears cascading down his face. My body shook, and I had to refrain from wanting to run over to grab him into a hug. I hated that I still wanted to protect him after the pain he had put me through.

"Any closing remarks before I sentence the defendant?" Judge Brown asked.

"My client would like to say something, if that is okay with you Your Honor?" my lawyer asked. She knew what I was about to do, and she disagreed with it.

"I'll allow it."

I stood up and tugged at my slacks to get them from out of my crotch. I started, "I just wanted to say that, and I might sound crazy, Shameek is a good person. He has mentioned his battle with DID and I ask Your Honor that instead of sending him to prison, send him to a long term, inpatient care. Granted, he did those things to me, but he wasn't himself. And I know and understand that. I am not making an excuse for him, but Your Honor, he needs help to learn how to keep his DID under control. That is all and thank you, Your Honor."

My lawyer sideeyed me as I took my seat next to her. When I told her that I didn't want to see him in jail, she told me that he deserved to be in a jail. If Judge Brown didn't ask for closing remarks, he would have had a fiftyfifty chance. Judge Brown looked down at me, silently asking if I was sure.

"We'll take a ten minute recess. Mrs. Simmons I would like to speak with you in my chambers," Judge Brown spoke. The bailiff walked over to Sheek and began to walk him to the back as we made our way out of the courtroom.

"I'm sorry, Korrin. I love you!" Sheek yelled before the doors closed. My head hung low as we waited in the halls.

Keesha approached me and rubbed my back. Angel came over and said, "It's going to be okay."

I wish that was the truth. How do I be strong for not only myself, but my children as well? Getting myself out of the depression was only half of the battle. Four months could easily happen again, but stay longer. Just keep yourself busy, I coached myself. Ten minutes passed, and we were allowed in the courtroom.

"As much as I don't want to do this sentencing, Ms. Richards, I believe that I would have to agree with you. Mr. Scott has not had the proper counseling or care to know and understand how to take care of his illness. I hereby sentence Mr. Scott to a year of inpatient care at Ellis Residential and Rehabilitation Center. Following his release, you will continue outpatient counseling and there is an indefinite stay away order in place. Mr. Scott, if you come anywhere near Ms. Richards, you will be sent to jail. Do you understand, Mr. Scott?"

"Yes, Your Honor," Sheek answered.

"You are set to be released tomorrow and straight from Schenectady County Jail, you will go to Ellis. In addition, you will also be placed on five years' probation."

"Thank you, Your Honor," Sheek responded.

"Don't thank me. Thank Ms. Richards. I already had my sentencing once I saw those pictures. Mr. Scott, I hope that you receive the help that you need through these services. Court is dismissed."

The bailiff walked over to Sheek and led him back through the doors that led to the holding cells. Keesha grabbed my hand and helped me up. We walked out of the courtroom, and all the while, I prayed that he got the help and stuck to it.

"Thank God it's over. You don't have to see him ever again and we can help you get through this day by day," Keesha mentioned.

I wanted to believe this. I truly did, but I knew deep down this wasn't the end.

"Keesha, I don't know if I can believe that. He's gonna get out of that rehab and could possibly come back." I was beginning to panic. It became too hard for me to breathe and dots began to become visible in my line of vision. I reached out to grab something or someone because I knew I was going to fall.

"Oh my God! Korrin! Somebody call an ambulance!" Thomasina yelled. It was the last thing I heard before I fell completely and comfortably into darkness.

***

I felt my eyes flutter as I tried to open them. Getting them to open without slamming them shut again, due to the intensity of the bright lights, was a task in itself. There was an I.V. stuck in my arm and my entire body felt weak. Keesha was sitting in the only chair available and was the only one in the room. She was sleeping with her mouth wide open. I reached for the remote that had the call bell attached to it and I pressed it.

Within thirty seconds later, a nurse appeared in the doorway. She made her way to my bed and asked if I was okay.

"Yes, I am. I'm just confused as to what happened. I just remembered leaving from out of the courtroom," I said. I ran my hand across my forehead due to a massive headache.

"From what your sister told us, she said that you passed out. She caught you, so you were lucky enough to not have banged your head on anything."

"So why so I have such a bad headache? These lights hurt my eyes."

The nurse walked to the wall and dimmed the lights down. She said, "Well, you were severely dehydrated. I'll go get the doctor so that you can speak with him. Just let me make sure that your vitals are good."

By this time, Keesha had woken up and was stalking her way over to me as if she was a mother hen. The nurse wore a simple smile on her face while she finished up what she was doing.

"Why haven't you been eating right or staying hydrated? I thought you were out of that depression stage," Keesha stated.

"Once you have depression, it doesn't go away. Somebody could be depressed and not know it and just go about life like it's nothing. This thing with Sheek has put me there and while I may not be stuck in bed on a daily and crying my eyes out, I am still trying to live through the fact that someone I loved beat me so bad that I could have died. I haven't eaten much but I do eat. I guess today just was the last straw," I explained as best as I could.

"I'm sorry. I just worry about you."

"I know, and I appreciate it, truly I do. I'm going to get through this, but it's going to take some time."

"Hello, Ms. Richards. You gave us quite a scare there. I'm Dr. Petersick. How are you feeling?" the doctor asked while hooking his stethoscope to his ears.

"I feel a little bit better. I'm quite hungry and need to go see my kids. Which brings me to the question, when will I be released?"

"Well, your vitals and good and stable, so in the next half hour you can go home. I must advise you, though, if you want to deliver a healthy baby, you must eat and stay healthy."

Keesha's eyes ballooned and she said, "Excuse me? Run that back again."

Dr. Petersick looked between Keesha and me. He asked, "You didn't know?"

Closing my eyes for a second, I opened them and said, "I knew. She didn't."

"I'm sorry if I ruined the surprise. I'll go and get your discharge papers." He knew he fucked up and left the room, so he didn't feel any heat.

"How long did you know?" Keesha asked as soon as the room was clear.

"For about two months."

"Why didn't you say anything?"

"Because I was unclear as to what I wanted to do. You know that I don't believe in abortions. But I didn't want to bring a baby in the world who has an abusive father. I think that was another reason why I was trying to tell you that this isn't over. He's going to find out that I'm pregnant and want to be there. And I don't want that to happen, so I battled with myself and came close to getting an abortion. I made it to the clinic and thought about the kids.

"I was so strong behind keeping them, never thought about abortion, so why would I or should I do such a thing to this baby? It's not its fault that its father has a mental illness. And

154

that is no excuse as to why I should get rid of this baby. The kids asked for years for another sibling. I can't do that to them," I said. The tears fell freely. I was upset with myself that I would even thinking about some shit like that.

Keesha walked closer to the bed and wrapped her arms around me. Her tears dropped onto my forehead as she comforted me and told me things were going to be alright. The nurse walked in, interrupting out kumbaya moment, and placed my release papers onto the table.

"Before I go, and maybe I'm overstepping my boundaries, but this isn't the end for you, sweetie. This could be a new beginning. You are strong. You're a woman, for God's sake. You got this and everything else that will come in the future. Get well, and make sure that you take care of yourself and this baby growing in you. It's a blessing," the nurse said. With a warm smile, she turned and walked out of the room.

She didn't overstep her boundaries, and little did she know, every word that she said, I needed to hear it. My spirit was so broken from all that I had gone through. That pickmeup she gave me, gave me all that I got my shit together and to never ignore the red flags ever again.

Mimi

156

Chapter Nineteen

Eight Months Pregnant

Finally surfaced above the downs
Feeling her boldest, she came around
'Cause she's a GODDESS, finally saw this

The sound of my cell phone vibrating against my night stand woke me from the nap that I managed to slip into. The Saturday afternoon sun peeked through my curtains as I rubbed the sleep from my eyes. Surprisingly, the kids were quiet. Grabbing my phone, I opened it up to see who it was that called me. I was Angel.

Since I met Angel, she was everything her name was. Angel became a dear friend to me and countless nights, she came through and listened to me. There was one night where I was crying so hard that I barely was able to speak. Keeping me on the phone, she came to my house and sat with me. I felt like I wasn't going to make it. My thoughts and flashbacks didn't help and at moments I've had several thoughts of just ending it. As I would be contemplating on killing myself and this baby, one of the kids would come inside of my room and prove to me that while I felt this way, I had more than enough reason as to why I needed to be here. It was selfish of me to think these things knowing that my children had nobody else but me. Losing me would cause them to lose their minds, and that is something that I wasn't going to allow them to go through.

Climbing out of the bed, I walked out of my room to use the bathroom and search for the kids. Passing by the living room, I noticed they were sitting on the couches with books in their hands. Julian looked up and noticed me first.

"Oh hey, Mom," he spoke.

"Hey what y'all doing?" I asked.

Matthew spoke up, "You were taking a nap and we didn't want to wake you up. We know that you get tired a lot with the new baby in your stomach and we wanted you to get your rest."

A smile appeared on my face and my heart melted. I responded, "I appreciate y'all so much. Let me use the bathroom and return this phone call to Miss Angel, and I will join y'all."

"Yay!" Julian yelled.

I rushed to use the bathroom and brush my teeth. I made it back to my room and placed the call to Angel. She picked up on the second ring.

"Hello, Miss Lady. How are you today?" she asked through the phone.

"I'm better today. How are you?"

"Chile, I'm always amazing. I'm just doing some shopping."

"Shopping?"

"Yes, tomorrow is my annual domestic violence awareness luncheon and I needed to pick up a few things."

"Oh. You never told me about those. What do you do?"

"We bring awareness to domestic violence while eating lunch and drinking tea. We raise money and split what we raise to the local domestic violence shelters."

"That is so dope."

Angel got quiet for a split second and then asked, "I know this may be too much to ask, but beside myself, there are three more women who share their stories. We have two new women that are sharing their stories. Would you like to share yours?"

My heart leaped into my throat. I didn't know if I was ready for that. My mouth had gone dry and I found it hard to speak. My mind raced, and I couldn't help but to think I wouldn't be able to do it. But what if your story help saves another woman? I thought. The "conversation" that I had with Shan resurfaced in my mind and I pushed my selfish thoughts to the side. Tuning back in, I realized that Angel was still rambling.

"Okay. I'll do it," I said, stopping her in midsentence.

"Really."

"Yes. When I had that mishap with his sister, I said that I would make sure that women knew everything about domestic violence. I'll do it. Besides, you've done so much for me and this is the least I could do to show you how much I appreciate you."

Angel squealed with excitement as she continuously thanked me. Giggling at her silliness, I told her to text me the address and if there was a special dress code that I should stick to.

After I hung up with her, I texted Keesha to see if she would watch the kids so that I could attend. Of course she agreed. Feeling better than ever, I made my way into the living room and cuddled up with the kids on the couch and read with them.

***

The next day, I woke up to get ready for Angel's luncheon. My nerves were getting the best of me and the baby was constantly flipping around in my stomach. Not even food calmed this child down and I could only imagine how hyperactive this baby would be once it was born.

The night before, I had gotten my outfit together. I braided my hair down and placed a stocking cap over the braids to put my wig on. After I'd eaten, I hopped in the shower, then sat at my vanity waiting for my makeup artist to arrive. Moments later, the doorbell rang.

"Iyana, can you get that! That's just someone I hired to do my makeup!" I yelled from my room.

"Okay!" Iyana responded.

I should have gone to meet her, but moving around at eight months pregnant was a challenge. Iyana walked into my room with the makeup artist just as I was placing a shirt over my head.

"Hi, are you, Inve?" I asked.

"Yes, I am. Thank you for contacting Inveouslay to do your makeup," she said with a smile on her face.

I was scrolling on Facebook one day when I happened to see one of her videos. She was a true artist and I knew that one day I would need to contact her, so I saved her contact info. The best part was that she was only located a few miles from me.

"No, thank you for coming on such short notice."

"It's my pleasure. Let's get you started," Inve said with a smile.

During the fortyfive minutes that it took for her to beat my face, we made small talk. She told me how she got started getting into makeup. I let her know that I was going to spread the word on how good she was. When she was done I looked at myself in the mirror and was thoroughly pleased. She gave me a natural look with a red lip and nude eyeshadow.

"Thank you so much," I said, damn near in tears. I handed her the money she was charging me and a healthy tip. Why not? She did an amazing job and I wanted to show that not only did I appreciate her coming on short notice, but also for transforming my fat pregnant face into something you would see in a magazine. With a smile, I walked her out, making sure to thank her one more time.

Escaping to my room, I started to get dressed. A few months ago I purchased a dress that was too large for my small frame due to me barely eating after the sentencing of Sheek. It was a black strapless dress with crisscross lace in the back. It was floor length with a side split in the front. I was afraid that maybe my belly had gotten so big that the dress couldn't fit, but the stretchy material proved me wrong. The shoes I chose to wear were gold opened Gianni Bini sixinch stiletto heels crystal ankle detail that would peep out of the split with every step I took. I put on my four diamond bangles with diamond stud earrings and a tear drop diamond necklace. My jet-black bob wig completed my look and I was more than happy with it.

"Bitch, you going to a luncheon or you going on a date? 'Cause bitch you look the fuck good!" Keesha screamed excitedly.

Giggling, I looked at her and asked, "You don't think this is too much?"

"Oh no, honey. You look like you're trying to make a statement. And it's loud and clear. You look amazing. Belly and all."

"I'm nervous. What if they think my dress is too revealing?"

Keesha looked at me with a serious look and pushed some hair from my face and said, "It doesn't matter what people say. You look good and you should own that. You are showing a confidence in you that so many women wish that they could show off. And that is not in a bad way. Just that some women don't have the confidence. Listen, you wear that dress and you wear it proud. This could be your 'I – lived – through – the –

worst – storm – possible – and – I – am – strong – enough – to – keep – pushing – through' dress."

Even though I doubted myself, Keesha made valid points. I checked the time and saw that I was running a little bit behind. I grabbed my bejeweled crossbody purse, threw some money inside, my lip gloss, and my phone after I called for an Uber. When my Uber arrived, I told Keesha and the kids that I would see them in a little while and I left.

My stomach fluttered with nervousness as we got closer and closer to my destination. Twenty minutes later, I arrived at the Rainbow Center in Troy. It was a center that was in Fallon Apartments and was, on a normal day, used as an afterschool program for the children in the housing complex. After thanking my driver, I made my way inside and looked around for Angel. She was the only one that I would know there and the more I didn't see her, the more I began to feel out of my element.

"Oh my God! Korrin!" I heard Angel squeal from behind me. I spun around and was so damn glad to see her in a similarlooking dress that I had on except hers was red with thick straps on the shoulder and she didn't have a split. She had on black pumps and she wore her hair in a bun on the nape of her neck.

"Hey, Angel. You look good as hell too," I complimented. And it was the truth. She looked damn good.

"Me? No, look at you. You are wearing the hell out of the dress, and look how big your belly has grown."

"I do have one more month, and I'm pretty sure that I'm going to get bigger."

"You still don't know what you are having?"

"No. I just want to make sure that whatever it is, it's healthy," Korrin expressed

Angel giggled and said, "A healthy baby is all that matters. Come with me and let me introduce you to a few of the ladies."

The room was big. There was a makeshift stage at the front and white chairs lined up neatly with purple sashes tried into bows. Purple and white balloons decorated the room. There was a table with a purple table cloth across it and triangle shaped sandwiches were on display along with cookies and cake. My stomach grumbled and as we walked past the table, I grabbed a tuna sandwich and kept walking.

We approached two women with their backs turned. They were both dressed in simple dresses and heels. One woman had big curly goldenbrown hair and the other woman wore her hair straight down her back.

"Quinn and Mah'lani, I would like to introduce you to someone," Angel spoke.

They turned around and my mouth dropped at their beauty. I couldn't even imagine them being abused, but I had to remind myself that it could happen to anyone.

"This is Korrin. She is going to be speaking with you ladies tonight. She just went through a similar situation with her abuser and is wanting to share her story," Angel spoke.

"It's nice to meet you," Quinn spoke to me.

Mah'lani nodded her head in agreement and as I reached to shake their hands, they took each one of my sides, careful of my belly, and embraced me into a hug. Of course I was in shock but when they hugged me, I knew that it was from a good place. When they let me go, I looked for Angel, but she had disappeared. Quinn and Mah'lani held a conversation with me and it felt like we had known each other for years with the way we bonded and laughed.

Soon enough, everyone took their seats, and me, Quinn, and Mah'lani took seats at the front. Angel took to the stage and began to introduce herself and tell her story.

Over the months that I've grown to know Angel, she told me bits and pieces of her story but today, she went deep into detail. She said that she was married to a very wellknown criminal lawyer for six years. They were together collectively for ten years. The first four years before they wed, she described as being magical. He treated her like a queen. There were lavish gifts, dates, and she had even moved into his lavish condo after being with him for six months. She mentioned that she saw the red flags, but decided to ignore them. She was blinded by his money, and soon enough she realized that he had stopped her from hanging from her friends to hang with his. Even at that point she should have caught on, but she didn't.

They ended up getting married and before the ink dried on the marriage license, his ultimate colors started to come out. When things wouldn't go his way, whatever was in his sight, he would break. That graduated to him pinching her skin, slapping her if he felt like she embarrassed him while they were out, and then ultimately led him to beating her down to the ground almost on an everyday basis. It would be something that was so simple like his food not being hot enough and he was beating her down for that. I was no longer able to hold back my tears and as I peeked around the room. Most of the women in the room had tearstained cheeks.

Tuning back into what Angel was saying, she said that her last straw as when he took her to the Bahamas on what was an "I'm – sorry – it – won't – happen – again" trip. There were a lot of those. The first day they had gotten there was good. They arrived at eight o' clock in the morning, took a nap, and were having lunch on the patio of one of the restaurants at the hotel. After lunch, they had a few drinks on the beach while for once they talked without yelling at each other. Angel said that she felt hope for them but deep down, she knew that it wouldn't last long. After the beach, he took Angel shopping, buying her several beautiful dresses, jewelry, and shoes.

They ate dinner in the hotel restaurant and then returned to their room. Angel explained that here was fire between them that she hadn't felt in a long time. For two hours, he made sure to take care of her body. When they were done, several orgasms later, she was knocked out.

It wasn't until she heard a baby crying that she realized she had fallen asleep. It was muffled due to the sound coming through the wall. Angel had woken up and when she didn't feel her husband next to her, she got up to check the suite. He was nowhere to be found. She called his cell phone, which just vibrated on the night stand next to the bed. The shrill of the baby crying felt like it was digging holes into her brain. She figured that she would knock on the door to see if there was anything that she could do to help.

She was more than shocked to see her husband open the door in his boxers, no less. Angel said she was stuck in that moment when a woman walked up behind him in a robe with just her panties on, and was holding the baby while it fed from her breast. The woman knew nothing of Angel because as Angel walked away back to the room, she heard her asking who she was.

Angel had started packing her things. Her husband followed her to the room and had the nerve to be mad at her for knocking on the door. She started to explain to him why she did and stopped. She came to the realization that not only was he cheating, but he had a baby on her. One minute she was packing her things and the next she was flying across the bed. He pushed her and was on top of her pummeling her face and body with his fists. She was beaten so badly that she was close to death and the only thing that saved her was the woman, his baby mother, calling hotel security. He was arrested, and she was taken to the hospital. While she was in the hospital for two weeks recovering, they shipped him back to the United States. Angel didn't bother to go to their condo. Everything she owned she left there and went to stay with her sister. While there, she began the divorce and order of protection process.

When Angel was done, there was not a dry eye in that room and when she walked off the stage, every woman in that room stood up and applauded her. Next was Mah'lani.

Mah'lani thought she had found the love of her life, but that quickly changed when her boyfriend began to lie to her. Soon enough, the abuse began. She was a virgin when she met him, and he accepted that part of her. He never pushed her into having sex with him. It began with a lie about his mother being dead, when in fact she was alive and taking care of his daughter that he failed to mention. She felt that him having a child was nothing major to have to hide. After all, he knew that she couldn't have children. He often would put her down about her weight and say that the reason why she couldn't have children was because she was so big, even though she told him it was because of her having her fallopian tubes removed when she was just seventeen years old.

Her breaking point was a dream that Dominic killed her. She was at this point playing mommy to his daughter. The mother that he had said died, dropped his daughter off, and said that she was no longer taking care of her. His daughter's mother basically left her with his mom and went about her life. With her relationship with Dominic being so rocky, his daughter quickly became the brightest thing in her world.

In the dream that she had, Dominic forced her to eat dog food and practically forced her to marry him. At the altar, the preacher had asked if anyone had to say anything. Several seconds passed and no one said anything. Mah'lani had told

Dominic that she couldn't marry him. His response was to shoot her.

When Mah'lani woke up, Dominic had just gotten in the house from drinking and he requested a beer. She gave it to him and put shoes on her and his daughter and left. She became friends with a guy that she worked with, her best friend, and thank God that night he was driving past and picked her up. She was just getting to know the guy when one night, they went out with her best friend and her boyfriend when the guy went out for a smoke and he ended up being killed. His murderer was still on the loose, but deep down Mah'lani felt that it was Dominic behind it. She now had full custody of his daughter and was trying to push for adoption. Dominic and his baby mother disappeared.

I'd never cried so hard in my life. The amount of shit that women put up with is sickening but also amazing to show just how strong we are. Women are often ridiculed for staying in an abusive relationship because they are weak, and it's not that. Women love so damn hard and see the best in people that we'd rather deal with what they are giving us at their worst. Most times we could leave and save ourselves and other times women die trying to justify that this sick person loves them. Mah'lani was applauded as well. Next was Quinn.

Quinn started by letting us know that because of what she went through, she started a business called Helping Her, which is a safe haven for abused women. She helps them with shelter, clothes, food, jobs, etc. She receives grants from the state to make this all possible and is looking forward to opening a woman's and children center.

Quinn watched her father abuse and kill her mother. She vowed that when she was ready to settle down, she would make sure that it didn't happen to her. Her boyfriend Jason was in the army when he found out that he was schizophrenic.

He would think she was saying something to him and he would begin the assault. As much as she said she didn't want what her mother had, she stayed. Jason cheated on her with her best friend, who was still smiling in her face, knowing what Quinn was going through. She'd had it bad and my heart went out to her as she choked up a few times while sharing. She thanked everyone for listening and thanked her man, who was Jason's best friend, and her daughter. Wiping her tears, she let everyone know that if we knew anyone that needed help, Helping Her was open six days a week and there was a twentyfourhour phone service. Applause rang out for Quinn as well, and the realization that I had to go next made me sick to my stomach.

Angel walked over to me and took my sweaty hand into hers and forced me to look into her eyes. With unspoken words, she let me know that everything would be okay. I'd told this story a handful of times, so why was I so nervous about it? 'Cause this is a room full of strangers, my mind yelled at me. I thought about the torment Quinn, Angel, and Mah'lani must have gone through. I sucked it up. Angel helped me from my seat and helped me onto the stage. Before I knew it, I was speaking my truth, bringing tears to these women and accepting their shouts of "take your time" and "it gets easier". Sure, I've had friends who always supported me, but never have I experienced a room full of women that exuded so much powerful and positive energy.

By the time I was done, the makeup that Inve had placed on my face was tearstained and was spilling onto my dress in drops. I looked an utter mess and I had begun to feel sick. Angel helped me down from the makeshift stage. I excused myself and headed to the bathroom to make myself somewhat presentable. After releasing myself, I looked in the mirror and decided to take the makeup off. I looked down at my phone and it was only going on four in the afternoon, but I needed to go home and lie down. I called for an Uber and went to go look for Angel, who was off in the corner giving a hug to one of the women that attended the luncheon.

"Excuse me, Angel. I was just coming to let you know that I was going to head out. I'm not feeling too well," I mentioned as I approached her.

"Are you okay?" Angel asked, reaching to place her hand on my belly.

"Yes, I'm just a little nauseous and dizzy. I'll text you to let you know that I made it home."

"Please do." She reached over and gave me a hug and a kiss on the cheek.

I waved at the other women as I left and climbed into my awaiting Uber, headed home.

Mimi

Chapter Twenty

The first time I saw you
I knew my life had changed
I would've been done and gone
But I found purpose when I brought you home

My drive home was nice and peaceful, and I felt like I was a new person. Although I had gotten sick and had to leave, hearing the stories of several women who went through something similar, made me had an outlook on life. The need for me to help had grown, and I knew that I had to do everything to help as many women that I could.

I arrived at my house, thanked my Uber driver, and walked to my door. My thoughts were so engrossed in the luncheon that I never heard someone walk up behind me. I was grabbed from behind with a hand over my mouth and then there was pain in my lower and top part of my stomach. The assault only lasted for a few seconds, but it seemed like a lifetime. The assailant ran away as I dropped to the ground. My hand instinctively touched my stomach and I felt the warm liquid that was my own blood.

"Keeshaaaaaaa!" I yelled.

Seconds later she was at the door with wide eyes. The kids were standing behind her watching on in horror. The baby was moving so much in my belly and I knew it was reacting to my panic. Keesha yelled for Malcolm to go get a towel and instructed Iyana to call 911.

"It's going to be okay," Keesha said to me as she used the towel to stop me from bleeding. By it being my stomach, she was trying her best to not harm the baby.

"Keesha, my baby," I cried. My hot tears streamed down my face. I heard the sirens in the distance, but time felt like it was slowing down. God, please protect my baby, I prayed over and over.

The ambulance arrived, and the time sped up. I was being lifted onto the stretcher and placed in the ambulance.

"Korrin, I'll be there as soon as I can, I'll call Angel to go for now, but I'll be there soon," I heard Keesha say.

There was an oxygen mask placed over my face and an I.V. hooked to my arm. The wail of the siren was deafening, The EMT's were asking me several questions that I'm sure that I answered, but I didn't know if they were correct or not. The only thing that was running through my mind was if the baby was okay.

We arrived at the hospital, where they wheeled me in and were yelling my stats. The doctors wheeled me into the elevator and asked me how I was feeling. Amid everything, I heard them say they were going to prepare for an emergency CSection. The tears wouldn't stop flowing and my prayers kept flowing. We entered a room that was cold, and I saw nurses flying around the room. My dress was cut from my body, my shoes ripped from my feet, and my jewelry taken off.

"Ms. Richards, we are going to give you a local anesthesia and we are going to deliver your baby. You will be awake during the process and we'll have a blood transfusion connected to your I.V. Everything is going to be okay," the nurse spoke to me from behind a splash mask.

I nodded my head and she pulled a sheet up that didn't allow me to see the lower half of my body. The minutes felt like hours and all I prayed for was to hear my baby cries. That was the only thing I wanted to hear. I allowed myself to get lost in the sound of the beeping of the machines until I heard the baby cry. My body shook as I became engrossed in the tears escaping my eyes.

"It's a girl!" the nurse yelled and held the baby over the sheet to show me my baby.

There she was screaming her head off with a head full of hair. But there was something off. On her arm, there was blood dripping onto me. My eyes looked on in horror and the nurse caught my reaction and moved the baby.

"Baby is cut!" was all I heard. And then I think I passed out.

***

I was now in a room with dim lights and the beeping sounds of the machines ringing in my ear. I could feel the puffiness of my eyes from all the crying I had done. For sure I looked like a hotass mess. My wig was taken off my head so all I had on was the stocking cap that was covering my braids. There was a knock on the door and Keesha, the kids, and Angel popped their heads into the room. The kids were the first to be by my bedside and I could tell that all of them, including Keesha and Angel, had been crying.

"Mommy, are you okay?" the kids asked in unison.

"Yes, I'm okay." I smiled with fresh new tears slipping from my eyes.

"Can we see the baby?" Julian asked innocently.

Nodding my head yes, I removed the blanket that was covering Cammi's face and moved her closer to the kids. They watched her as she sucked on her hand, the one that was wounded when I was attacked. They had stitched her arm up and wrapped a bandage around it. She was in so much pain and I could tell by the way she cried for hours – that was, until she got some milk in her system and calmly hiccupped herself to sleep. Iyana, Malcolm, and Julian looked at her in amazement and placed kisses on her forehead.

"She's beautiful," Angel choked out.

"Please don't cry. I've been crying for hours and I don't want to cry any more. Cammi is here and healthy and that's all that matters," I said.

"I can't help it."

Keesha interrupted while rolling her eyes in a playful way. She said, "She's been crying since I called her."

"Where's Dalila?"

"With her father downstairs. Your family is here and waiting for us to come back down so that they could see you. Tahjae is downstairs drunk and cutting the fuck up. You want her to come up?"

I sighed because this girl couldn't put the drink down if she wanted to. I said, "When you go back downstairs, just tell her that she won't be allowed in here if she don't get her shit together. I don't have the energy to deal with her shit right now."

"Okay. Me and Angel will go down and send them up. Everyone is here."

I nodded my head and watched as they walked out of the room. Five minutes later, each of my siblings filed into the room along with my mother. They all had frightened looks on their faces and no one said a word. They crowded around my bed and looked down at Cammi and that was what broke the silence. While everyone chatted amongst themselves.

Charles bent close to me. "Who the fuck did this?" he seethed.

"It was either Sheek's sister or his brother. I'm not sure which one, but I know for sure that it was one of them," I responded.

"You know where they stay?"

"No. But Charles, leave it be, please. I'm okay and so is Cammi, and that's what matters."

"Nah, fuck that, they need to get dealt with."

"Charles, I just want to move on from this. I know a woman that can help with finding me shelter and I will no longer be in that apartment. We will be fine. I promise. God can take care of them," I replied. And I was honest when I said I wanted to move on. I didn't want him getting in trouble because of me and he's in jail not enjoying his baby girl's life. What kind of sister would I be? Charles looked at me and I nodded my head to let him know that I was sure. He hugged me and placed a kiss on my forehead.

I sat back on the bed while I watched everyone fawn over Cammi. All seven of my mother's children were in the same room, not bickering, and getting along with one another. It sucked that I had to get hurt for this to happen but I, no less, was happy that they were here. I know my mother was too. This was not the end for me. This was my beginning.

Mimi

Epilogue

2019

I can make the days disappear
And I can erase the past
I can make the future shine bright
And I can make right now alright

The last year has been hard, but eventful. Connecting with Quinn after Cammi and I were released from the hospital has been the best decision that I could have ever made. Within two months, I was in a new apartment in Albany and transferred my job over to an Albany office. They gave me a year off for paid maternity leave and I couldn't have been more thankful for that. With the time off, I volunteered for Helping Her and got to meet a lot of amazing people.

The time for me to get back to work was winding down and I was preparing myself to have to send Cammi to daycare. I've never sent Iyanna, Malcolm, and Julian to daycare due to me always being at home when they were young, and the butterflies that I would get at just the thought of sending her to one made me sick.

We were days away from throwing Cammi her first birthday party and for months, there was something that was unsettling with me. I knew what it was, but I hated to have to be the one to do it. Keesha had taken the kids out to enjoy ice cream and the park, giving me a break, and I laid in bed going over the words that I wanted to tell my sister. She was going to be arriving soon and I was nervous. Nervous because she could be cool or come out of a bag on me. I only hoped that it would be her keeping her cool. The doorbell ringing broke me out of my thoughts as I got up to go open the door.

"I hate that you now live on the second floor. I be tired as shit walking up those stairs," Tahjae said, out of breath.

I laughed and said, "Do you want some water while you catch your breath?"

"Hell yeah, bitch, I'm about to die."

I laughed all the way to kitchen and grabbed her a bottle of water. Heading back, I decided to turn back around and get me one as well. Tahjae made herself comfortable on the couch as I handed her the bottle and I did the same on my other couch.

"You said that you wanted to talk to me about something, what's up?" she asked. That was one thing about sober Tahjae. She was always straightforward and to the point.

I fidgeted in my seat and cleared my throat. I began, "Yeah, I did. A while ago, you said something that haunts me. You had said that I always take up for other people, but never for you."

"Really? I don't remember saying that."

"Well, it was a while ago for one and two, you weren't sober when you said it."

"I didn't mean it. You know, that right?" she said, scooting to the edge of the couch.

"I wish that you didn't, but usually a drunk tongue speak a sober mind and I'm okay with that. You were right, but I was heated in the moment and didn't want to admit that. I had months to think this over and when I got stabbed while pregnant with Cammi, I had so much time to think about the underlying issues of our family. That day was the first time in years that all seven of us were in a room without drama."

Tahjae looked at me and became defensive. "I hope you not saying that the drama in this family is because of me, because just me alone cannot be the cause of this dysfunction."

178

"No, Tahjae, I just need you to listen to me and keep an open mind. We have our own responsibilities for this family being so dysfunctional, but that's not what I'm talking about. I think that over the years your drinking has become more excessive and I want to help you."

Tahjae looked at me in shock. Then she laughed, a hearty Ijustsaidthefunniestjoke laugh. She said, "You cannot be serious! Oh my God, you are serious. Y'all niggas are the reason why I drink so fucking much! Is this an intervention of some sort? Is everybody else going to jump out of rooms and agree with you and send me to some rehab?"

I sighed because I knew this was going to happen. I looked at her from the couch and said, "Tahjae, this isn't an intervention, no one is sending you to rehab, this is just me talking to you. I don't want to argue with anything. My life flashed before my eyes while I was laid up in that ambulance and the only thing that I thought about was you."

"Me?" she questioned. She was pacing and had stopped.

"Yes, you. And the reason why was because when we were young, we were the closest of Mommy's kids and over the years, I don't know where we went wrong. I know that if I would have died, you would have been lost and I'm glad that I was giving a second chance to be able to even sit here and have this conversation with you." Oh fuck, here comes the tears.

"Who put you up to this?" she asked.

"No one, Tahjae. Do you know that you could die from alcoholism? And I wish that you would join a rehab, but I know you won't. I just want my baby sister back so that we can work on this relationship and hope that the rest of the family follows."

Tahjae looked at me like I was crazy. Her arms hung by her sides as she walked over to me and hugged me. She said, "You're ugly when you cry, so can you please stop."

Pushing her off me, she continued, "Listen, I know I'm not perfect and I don't claim to be but changing has been on my mind for the longest time. I was tired of going to bed hungover to have to wake up and drink the last thing I was drinking to get rid of the hang over. I hated walking the streets, even sober, smelling like a winery. Besides, I have a reason as to not drink anymore. Well, at least for a while."

I wiped my tears from my face. I looked at her and she had tears streaming from her eyes as well. I said, "What is that?"

"You're gonna be an aunt again," she said with a smile on her face.

"No way! No fucking way! You didn't want kids! What the fuck? Is it a boy or girl?"

"Relax!" she shouted while giggling. I placed my hand on her stomach, and I should have known. Her stomach, which is usually flat, was now a small pudge.

"Okay. Who's the father?" I asked. For the longest she was only messing with the dude in jail. He wasn't home yet, so this mystery man was throwing me for a loop.

"My husband."

My mouth dropped as she flashed her ring in my face. The ring was fucking beautiful. There was a pink diamond that sat on top a cluster of smaller diamonds. Her smile was bright and wide as she giggled and did the "Baby Mama" dance.

"Your what? When the fuck did you get married?" I was flabbergasted. Tahjae can't hold water, so how she kept this a secret, I couldn't even begin to think.

Honk! Honk! Honkkkkkkkk!

"That's him right now. I told him to meet me over here 'cause we are going to go celebrate the news of the baby.

Don't tell nobody 'cause I want to be the one to tell everyone. Come downstairs to meet him. He's real sweet and I'm happy to have met him. We've only been married a couple of months, but after Sheek was sent to that rehab, I had met him, and we been rocking since."

"Tahjae, you barely know him. Are you sure about this?"

"Asking if I'm sure is a little too late. I've already married him." She giggled.

I took a good look at Tahjae and she was genuinely happy. I didn't want to be the one to burst her bubble, so I decided to be happy for her. She needed me to be her support because Lord knows how judgmental my family would be when they find out.

"Okay, okay, okay. I'll meet him. Let me put some shoes on my feet."

Running into my room, I put on my Nike slides and followed Tahjae downstairs. There was something funny going on with this situation, and I felt it in my stomach. When we got downstairs, Tahjae happily bounced to his car and I could hear her tell him to get out the car to meet me. The car door swung open and his head popped out facing the other direction. He was wearing a black and red fitted hat with a black shirt. Slowly – well, it felt like it was slow— he turned toward me, and my mouth dropped. No this can't be happening. Tahjae can't be this stupid, I thought.

"Sean," I whispered. The beam on Tahjae's face turned into a mask of taunting, but maybe that was just my mind registering it that way. I know she'd seen him only once at my graduation and I don't know if she remembered what he looked like, but this couldn't be happening. I knew by the smile on Sean's face that he knew that I knew what he did was on purpose. What the fuck do I do? What the fuck is happening?

Mimi

The End!

Submission Guideline

Submit the first three chapters of your completed manuscript to ldpsubmissions@gmail.com, subject line: Your book's title. The manuscript must be in a .doc file and sent as an attachment. Document should be in Times New Roman, double spaced and in size 12 font. Also, provide your synopsis and full contact information. If sending multiple submissions, they must each be in a separate email.

Have a story but no way to send it electronically? You can still submit to LDP/Ca$h Presents. Send in the first three chapters, written or typed, of your completed manuscript to:

LDP: Submissions Dept
Po Box 870494
Mesquite, Tx 75187

DO NOT send original manuscript. Must be a duplicate.

Provide your synopsis and a cover letter containing your full contact information.

Thanks for considering LDP and Ca$h Presents.

Coming Soon from Lock Down Publications/Ca$h Presents

BOW DOWN TO MY GANGSTA

By **Ca$h**

TORN BETWEEN TWO

By **Coffee**

BLOOD STAINS OF A SHOTTA **III**

By **Jamaica**

STEADY MOBBIN **III**

By **Marcellus Allen**

BLOOD OF A BOSS **VI**

SHADOWS OF THE GAME II

By **Askari**

LOYAL TO THE GAME **IV**

By **T.J. & Jelissa**

A DOPEBOY'S PRAYER **II**

By **Eddie "Wolf" Lee**

IF LOVING YOU IS WRONG… **III**

By **Jelissa**

TRUE SAVAGE **VII**

MIDNIGHT CARTEL

DOPE BOY MAGIC

By **Chris Green**

BLAST FOR ME **III**

DUFFLE BAG CARTEL **IV**

HEARTLESS GOON **III**

A SAVAGE DOPEBOY II

By **Ghost**

A HUSTLER'S DECEIT III

KILL ZONE **II**

BAE BELONGS TO ME III

SOUL OF A MONSTER III

By **Aryanna**

THE COST OF LOYALTY **III**

By **Kweli**

THE SAVAGE LIFE II

By **J-Blunt**

KING OF NEW YORK V

COKE KINGS IV

BORN HEARTLESS III

By **T.J. Edwards**

GORILLAZ IN THE BAY V

De'Kari

THE STREETS ARE CALLING II

Duquie Wilson

KINGPIN KILLAZ IV

STREET KINGS III

PAID IN BLOOD III

CARTEL KILLAZ III

Hood Rich

SINS OF A HUSTLA II

ASAD

TRIGGADALE III

Elijah R. Freeman
KINGZ OF THE GAME V
Playa Ray
SLAUGHTER GANG IV
RUTHLESS HEART II
By Willie Slaughter
THE HEART OF A SAVAGE II
By Jibril Williams
FUK SHYT II
By Blakk Diamond
THE DOPEMAN'S BODYGAURD II
By Tranay Adams
TRAP GOD II
By Troublesome
YAYO II
A SHOOTER'S AMBITION II
By S. Allen
GHOST MOB
Stilloan Robinson
KINGPIN DREAMS
By Paper Boi Rari
CREAM
By Yolanda Moore
SON OF A DOPE FIEND II
By Renta
FOREVER GANGSTA II
By Adrian Dulan

LOYALTY AIN'T PROMISED

By Keith Williams

THE PRICE YOU PAY FOR LOVE

By Destiny Skai

THE LIFE OF A HOOD STAR

By Rashia Wilson

TOE TAGZ II

By Ah'Million

Available Now

RESTRAINING ORDER **I & II**

By **CA$II & Coffee**

LOVE KNOWS NO BOUNDARIES **I II & III**

By **Coffee**

RAISED AS A GOON I, II, III & IV

BRED BY THE SLUMS I, II, III

BLAST FOR ME I & II

ROTTEN TO THE CORE I II III

A BRONX TALE I, II, III

DUFFEL BAG CARTEL I II III

HEARTLESS GOON

A SAVAGE DOPEBOY

HEARTLESS GOON I II

By **Ghost**

LAY IT DOWN **I & II**

LAST OF A DYING BREED

BLOOD STAINS OF A SHOTTA I & II

By **Jamaica**

LOYAL TO THE GAME

LOYAL TO THE GAME II

LOYAL TO THE GAME III

LIFE OF SIN I, II III

By **TJ & Jelissa**

BLOODY COMMAS I & II

SKI MASK CARTEL I II & III

KING OF NEW YORK I II,III IV

RISE TO POWER I II III

COKE KINGS I II III

BORN HEARTLESS I II

By **T.J. Edwards**

IF LOVING HIM IS WRONG…I & II

LOVE ME EVEN WHEN IT HURTS I II III

By **Jelissa**

WHEN THE STREETS CLAP BACK I & II III

By **Jibril Williams**

A DISTINGUISHED THUG STOLE MY HEART I II & III

LOVE SHOULDN'T HURT I II III IV

RENEGADE BOYS I II III IV

By **Meesha**

A GANGSTER'S CODE I &, II III

A GANGSTER'S SYN I II III

THE SAVAGE LIFE

By J-Blunt

PUSH IT TO THE LIMIT

By **Bre' Hayes**

BLOOD OF A BOSS **I, II, III, IV, V**

SHADOWS OF THE GAME

By **Askari**

THE STREETS BLEED MURDER **I, II & III**

THE HEART OF A GANGSTA I II& III

By **Jerry Jackson**

CUM FOR ME

CUM FOR ME 2

CUM FOR ME 3

CUM FOR ME 4

CUM FOR ME 5

An **LDP Erotica Collaboration**

BRIDE OF A HUSTLA **I II & II**

THE FETTI GIRLS **I, II& III**

CORRUPTED BY A GANGSTA I, II III, IV

BLINDED BY HIS LOVE

By **Destiny Skai**

WHEN A GOOD GIRL GOES BAD

By **Adrienne**

THE COST OF LOYALTY I II

By Kweli

A GANGSTER'S REVENGE **I II III & IV**

THE BOSS MAN'S DAUGHTERS

THE BOSS MAN'S DAUGHTERS II

THE BOSSMAN'S DAUGHTERS III

THE BOSSMAN'S DAUGHTERS IV

THE BOSS MAN'S DAUGHTERS **V**

A SAVAGE LOVE **I & II**

BAE BELONGS TO ME I II

A HUSTLER'S DECEIT I, II, III

WHAT BAD BITCHES DO I, II, III

SOUL OF A MONSTER I II

KILL ZONE

By **Aryanna**

A KINGPIN'S AMBITON

A KINGPIN'S AMBITION **II**

I MURDER FOR THE DOUGH

By **Ambitious**

TRUE SAVAGE

TRUE SAVAGE II

TRUE SAVAGE **III**

TRUE SAVAGE **IV**

TRUE SAVAGE **V**

TRUE SAVAGE **VI**

By **Chris Green**

A DOPEBOY'S PRAYER

By **Eddie "Wolf" Lee**

THE KING CARTEL **I, II & III**

By **Frank Gresham**

THESE NIGGAS AIN'T LOYAL **I, II & III**

By **Nikki Tee**

GANGSTA SHYT **I II &III**

By **CATO**

THE ULTIMATE BETRAYAL

By **Phoenix**

BOSS'N UP **I , II & III**

By **Royal Nicole**

I LOVE YOU TO DEATH

By Destiny J

I RIDE FOR MY HITTA

I STILL RIDE FOR MY HITTA

By **Misty Holt**

LOVE & CHASIN' PAPER

By **Qay Crockett**

TO DIE IN VAIN

SINS OF A HUSTLA

By **ASAD**

BROOKLYN HUSTLAZ

By **Boogsy Morina**

BROOKLYN ON LOCK I & II

By **Sonovia**

GANGSTA CITY

By **Teddy Duke**

A DRUG KING AND HIS DIAMOND I & II III

A DOPEMAN'S RICHES

HER MAN, MINE'S TOO I, II

CASH MONEY HO'S

By Nicole Goosby

TRAPHOUSE KING **I II & III**

Mimi

KINGPIN KILLAZ I II III
STREET KINGS I II
PAID IN BLOOD **I II**
CARTEL KILLAZ I II
By **Hood Rich**
LIPSTICK KILLAH **I, II, III**
CRIME OF PASSION I II & III
By **Mimi**
STEADY MOBBN' **I, II, III**
By **Marcellus Allen**
WHO SHOT YA **I, II, III**
SON OF A DOPE FIEND
Renta
GORILLAZ IN THE BAY **I II III IV**
DE'KARI
TRIGGADALE I II
Elijah R. Freeman
GOD BLESS THE TRAPPERS I, II, III
THESE SCANDALOUS STREETS I, II, III
FEAR MY GANGSTA I, II, III
THESE STREETS DON'T LOVE NOBODY I, II
BURY ME A G I, II, III, IV, V
A GANGSTA'S EMPIRE I, II, III, IV
THE DOPEMAN'S BODYGAURD
Tranay Adams
THE STREETS ARE CALLING
Duquie Wilson

MARRIED TO A BOSS… I II III

By Destiny Skai & Chris Green

KINGZ OF THE GAME I II III IV

Playa Ray

SLAUGHTER GANG I II III

RUTHLESS HEART

By Willie Slaughter

THE HEART OF A SAVAGE

By Jibril Williams

FUK SHYT

By Blakk Diamond

DON'T F#CK WITH MY HEART I II

By Linnea

ADDICTED TO THE DRAMA I II III

By Jamila

YAYO

A SHOOTER'S AMBITION

By S. Allen

TRAP GOD

By Troublesome

FOREVER GANGSTA

By Adrian Dulan

TOE TAGZ

By Ah'Million

<u>BOOKS BY LDP'S CEO, CA$H</u>

<u>TRUST IN NO MAN</u>
<u>TRUST IN NO MAN 2</u>
<u>TRUST IN NO MAN 3</u>
<u>BONDED BY BLOOD</u>
<u>SHORTY GOT A THUG</u>
<u>THUGS CRY</u>
<u>THUGS CRY 2</u>
<u>THUGS CRY 3</u>
<u>TRUST NO BITCH</u>
<u>TRUST NO BITCH 2</u>
<u>TRUST NO BITCH 3</u>
<u>TIL MY CASKET DROPS</u>
<u>RESTRAINING ORDER</u>
<u>RESTRAINING ORDER 2</u>
<u>IN LOVE WITH A CONVICT</u>

<u>Coming Soon</u>
BONDED BY BLOOD 2
BOW DOWN TO MY GANGSTA

Crime of Passion 3